T0121753

Fourth Down and Murder

Susan Rose O'Leary

iUniverse, Inc.
New York   Bloomington

Copyright © 2009 by Susan Rose O'Leary

All rights reserved. No part of this book may be used
or reproduced by any means, graphic, electronic, or
mechanical, including photocopying, recording, taping or
by any information storage retrieval system without the
written permission of the publisher except in the case of brief
quotations embodied in critical articles and reviews.

iUniverse books may be ordered through booksellers or by contacting:

iUniverse
1663 Liberty Drive
Bloomington, IN 47403
www.iuniverse.com
1-800-Authors (1-800-288-4677)

Because of the dynamic nature of the Internet, any Web addresses or
links contained in this book may have changed since publication and may
no longer be valid. The views expressed in this work are solely those of
the author and do not necessarily reflect the views of the publisher, and
the publisher hereby disclaims any responsibility for them.

ISBN: 978-1-4401-8505-2 (sc)
ISBN: 978-1-4401-8507-6 (hc)
ISBN: 978-1-4401-8506-9 (ebook)

Library of Congress Control Number: 2009912503

Printed in the United States of America

iUniverse rev. date: 12/21/2009

This book is for everyone in my family, including my extended family. Without them, I would never have been able to come up with these characters that I love so much. I especially want to thank Bill, the love of my life. He always wanted me to write a book and, without his confidence in me, this book would never have occurred. So if anyone finds himself or herself as a character in this book, blame him.

Chapter 1

Sundays in the fall are reserved for football. Simple logic requires it. Everyone of sound mind knows that the world needs silence, respect, an ice-cold beer, and a great chair on these sacred days. I, luckily, have a significant other who recognizes my special needs on these revered occasions. Comfortably established in my chair, watching my modern gladiators on high-def, I can hear that D, my significant other, is bustling in the kitchen. The smells of delicious culinary concoctions are being prepared just to enhance my Sunday experience. I am indeed lucky and life is blessed until the annoyance of unnecessary communication rings.

"D, the blasted phone is ringing off the hook. Can you get it, babe? The game has started."

A few seconds and one down later, D stands before me with the phone and I know that once again a Sunday is blown. Another client, another felony, and another day that D or, as he is called by everyone else, Destin, is pissed that his gourmet delight will end up in the trash, and we will miss football nirvana because of work. So much for the passing thought that I lead a blessed and extraordinarily lucky life. It is not that I am completely damned or unlucky. I just have the wrong type of damn luck. But that's the life of a female P.I. with a significant other who is a hotshot criminal lawyer.

The name is Rhia, short for Rhiannon, an ultra-feminine name placed upon this poor girl by a mother who constantly dreamt of bygone times and knights in shining armor. Mother spent all of her free time with her nose in a romance novel of dubious historical value. I have been blessed with this name in respect of my mother's Irish-Welsh heritage. Rhiannon is the Celtic goddess of inspiration. For many a priestess, the name represents the religious aspects associated with the moon. Rhiannon was also the Welsh goddess of the horse. I guess the nomenclature fits. I like to spend time at the local track betting on the ponies and much to the dismay of D I have been known to moon miscreants who annoy me. I doubt that my mother thought I would take that interpretation of my romantic name. She always assumed that I would become an inspired ballerina or a glorious star on Broadway. I can tap dance my way around any crime scene once the police have taken me to task for being there illegally. Singing is just not my thing and definitely not in anyone's best interest. Once I touched the leather of a football, all girly future was lost. Throwing a perfect spiral sends a shiver of delight throughout my body. I'm not a gal made for pampering or play-acting. I was made for action.

My D loves me just the way I am. That is why I know he is highly intelligent and why I was drawn to him from the first meeting. He is smart enough to know perfection when he sees it. I am the yin to his yang or something Zen like that. My yin loves to throw to his yang and he has a yang that gets my soul and body every time. Add that D loves to cook gourmet-style and that I love to eat anything he creates, and we are in heaven. Don't get me wrong. I don't live with D just for the food and great sports talk. At almost six feet tall, a great muscled, yet lean body, he is a calm soul and knows just when to let loose with a great joke. His deep brown eyes and adorable smile send me into orbit. I even like his somewhat straight nose, a result of years playing every sport known to man. He is masculine perfection. At the end of a case, I like nothing better than a long, hot bath and a night spent in his arms while we yang away. That was the plan for this weekend until the damn phone rang and bliss got busted.

The annoying phone call concerned an acquaintance of D's. I must tell you that I have never liked girls with cute names. You know the type, the Tonyas and the Barbies. Or girls named after plants like Pansy or fruits like Peaches or Tangerine. Why is this an issue? Well, when you are with a stud like D, you don't like any girls but the girls with the cute names are especially dangerous. My philosophy is that if a girl has an unbelievably cute name, then they are definitely the type of girl that needs a man to take care of them. They appeal to the masculine pride. I am helpless woman; you are great big man here to rescue me. Thus, when D told me that the phone call was from Tangy, red flags went flipping through my brain.

Tangy is involved in a murder. My initial thought is that she won't be a problem for me anymore since she will probably be in jail. Watching me, D knew immediately what I am thinking and once again informed me that it is our responsibility to do the right thing. "Doing the right thing" is his favorite phrase and something he truly believes. If you do the right thing for others, they will respond in kind. This is some sort of karma thing he likes to quote. D is a wonderful man, yet sometimes he can be so naïve. While I see the ugly side of people and always expect the beast in them to appear, D sees the best even if they don't have a best side. Tangy told D that Todd had been found dead outside her front door and that the police are asking her a lot of questions. She is scared, does not know what to do, and needs help. D contends that he should help her since she has helped him several times in the past. Tangy works for the local pro football team. Tangy's help has been to get great tickets to some of the games for D. It never bothered me until I met Tangy and found out that she is a redheaded knockout. She has the long legs that I wish I had and a sleek body to go with it. She dresses to accentuate her assets and always made sure that the tickets came complete with what I call a "come hither" note.

Tangy wants D to help her so I quickly offer my services. I do have a few questions to ask her. I need to know more about her boyfriend and more about those free football tickets like why the free tickets are available only when I am out of town. And how did the dead body of her boyfriend end up outside her door? Did he blow his brains out in front of her door because he was brokenhearted or did she kill him and leave him outside her door because that was as far as she could drag the outgoing trash?

D is off to the police station to rescue and protect the damsel in distress. My questions for Tangy can wait. She will be at police headquarters for hours answering the questions that D allows her to answer. I intend to take myself off somewhere far more interesting. Tangy's apartment is my destination. A fresh murder waiting for me to solve is far more exciting than any police station. Plus, there is always the chance that the police have closed down their initial walkthrough of her apartment. I can spend several hours there going over all the evidence that the police always seem to miss and, with luck, I might catch the end of the football game on her TV set. She better have a quality TV. If I'm giving up my Sunday for her, the least Tangy can do is to provide a decent large plasma or flat screen. Then if I find the evidence to close this case quickly, D and I can still salvage what is left of the evening and hit one of our favorite restaurants on the way home. If this doesn't happen, well, no luck is also good. D will need me to do a full investigation, which means more money in my pocket. I will get to work closely with him. Anything that gets me close to my man, even bloody murder, means great karma for me.

Tangy's apartment is on the upscale side of town. Plenty of streetlights, brew pubs, and fancy shops where a cup of coffee costs five bucks. It also means a plethora of cops so safety will not be an issue. That always makes D happy. However, with the overpriced drinks and the profusion of cops come problems that may prove to be bigger than my safety and D's state of contentment. Upscale abundance means I'll have to deal with independent, small-town cops who have big-city, New York attitudes. Her apartment is really a condo or, as I like to call them, apartments for the upwardly mobile who are on their way to a "loft." I will have to park my old, beat-up Bronco, my Bertha, down the road so I won't upset the ambience of the neighborhood. Damn, I hate doing work in this area; this is why I don't do divorce cases. Upscale means uptight.

I'm hoping the neighbors will be typical snobs and stay out of my way so they won't complicate my arrival. A quiet but quick entry to the condo, then total peace while I search things that I'm not supposed to notice or touch would be ideal. I hope that Mike will be the cop at the door. He is old school and recently transferred to the smaller police department after a bad shoot in the big city of San Antonio. Some of his old comrades in the police force let it be known that politics were involved in the heavy-handed internal investigation of the shooting.

Mike was cleared, but he was too irritated by the procedural "bullshit" as he called it to stay in the big city. He joined what I refer to as his "high-society" police department. What else would you call a police department with luxury vehicles as squad cars? Mike still likes to call his own shots even if he is now in the upper echelon of society. I'm hoping that he won't mind cutting me a little slack. Maybe if I remind him that I was on his side in the shooting and bring him a couple of bagels to help him pass the time, he'll cut me a break. As I get out of the elevator in Tangy's building, I luck out. My karmic cloud or whatever you call it must be getting better as the day progresses because Mike is there.

"Hey, old man. How come they have a pro cop like you holding down the hallway? Are you trying to keep nosey neighbors away from the evidence? Let me guess your job is to keep down the chatter and gossip in this suburban oasis."

His response to me was classic old-school Mike. Most of it

can't be repeated in polite society, but the rest is just plain funny. I love Mike and I know that he has a soft spot for me. I'm about to find out how much of a soft spot it really is.

Chapter 2

Mike is standing in the hallway just in front of where Todd was found. Thanks to the chalk outline on the floor, the exact spot where Tangy discovered Todd was easy to locate. Dried pools of blood and remnants of brain matter on the wall help to identify it as the kill zone. The coroner has already picked up the body, so I will have to get my interpretation of what happened from the blood splatter and whatever leftovers I can find and Mike, of course.

"Tell me, Mike. Were you the first one to arrive?" I ask casually, hoping Mike will freely divulge all the good stuff.

"Yeah, I got the call and was only a few blocks away. Found some guy slouched half on the floor and half against the wall. Had a funny, surprised look on his face and a great big hole where the side of his head had been," replied Mike in his typical been-there, done-that demeanor. It seems that Mike has seen just about everything in his career.

"Did the police find the weapon that killed him?"

"No, Rhia -- and I haven't heard anything back. The detectives had us interview all the occupants of the condos, but there are no witnesses. It must have been fast, neat, and quiet. Why are you here? Just for fun? Or are you helping your boyfriend protect the rights of his client or should I say murderer? Or are you here to check out the apartment for you and D? Thinking about moving out of your little cottage in the 'burbs? Hoping to get Tangy's place if she gets thrown out, are you? Own up to it, Rhia. You are in the mood to move to a more impressive zip code, right?"

That's Mike. Old school, everyone is guilty until we can prove him or her innocent.

"Mike, let's skip the small talk and the digs about the suburb, and let me into the condo. I promise not to touch anything."

"Yeah, right! I've heard that before so be extra careful and touch nothing. I don't want to get into trouble with these yuppie cops, because one wrong word from their mouths and they will feel my fist there before they finish their sentence. Then there goes retirement and I've only got five more years. Try to keep your illegal activities to a minimum, will ya? I hate it when I have to burn favors to get your ass out of deep shit."

I tell Mike that I can just feel the love growing between us and start to enter the condo.

"Hey, Rhia," Mike shouts. "You've got till I finish my bagels."

Count on good old Mike to add a time limit to my visit. I have no intention of arguing with Mike over a couple of seconds. I'd have better luck with a wall. Mike is a big man. He's been around a long time and has the stomach and thin hair to prove it but never underestimate him. If I get caught in a fight, I want Mike on my side even if he is five years from retirement. He is built like a tank and has fists that can break a criminal's face with one hit. Mike doesn't sugarcoat anything and that includes taking down a suspect. Clobber him first and ask questions later. I said he graduated from the old school. Damn, I should have brought more bagels. Mike will go through the few mini bagels that I brought faster than a driver can complete a lap at the Indy 500. This will have to be a quick search and look and there goes the TV and the end of the game. I am starting to like Tangy less and less.

I thought Tangy's condo was upscale, but the inside blows my mind. How can a woman live this way? My first impression is that she lives alone. Whoever this Todd person was, he definitely was not her live-in boyfriend. Not unless he was kinky and into fur — and pink synthetic fur at that. Everywhere I look, all I see is pink. I start laughing, which is an odd thing to do at a murder scene, but all I can think of is my D living here and wearing a pink apron while cooking out of pink pans and watching sports on an unbelievable Disney princess-style pink TV. My stomach starts to growl and I am reminded that the phone call we received from Tangy occurred before we ate D's gourmet dinner. Missing dinner and surrounded by pink, I find myself with a sudden headache and a strange craving for cotton candy.

Taking my time in Tangy's pink condo is not as interesting as I thought it would be. I check her files and papers. Nothing. I check her desk. Nothing. I look under the bed, in the freezer, and inside the back of the toilet bowl. I check all of the usual hiding places and get absolutely nothing. There is no evidence to indicate that Tangy and Todd were involved in anything shady. No drugs, no pictures that could be used to blackmail someone, no guns, nothing. I guess the police forensic team has already cleared out anything of interest. The pink is starting to infiltrate the recesses of my brain, indicating that it might be time to leave. I turn to leave and walk to the door of the apartment when I catch a glance at a picture frame out of place.

First, Tangy's pink palace was immaculate. Nothing was out of place even after the police forensic team finished. Yet, something about the way the frame is hanging calls me. Once the picture frame is open, I get what I hope will be the first break and piece of evidence that might help me understand exactly what happened here tonight. The paper says three things: The names of Todd and Tangy, the number 1.5 million, and a time and place for delivery. I'm pleased to finally have something of substance. It is pure instinct that makes me believe that this definitely needs to be investigated. I just have to make sure that D doesn't discover that I removed a piece of evidence from the crime scene. For some reason, it drives D to distraction when I do these things. I don't think it should be a deal breaker. The deal being that I will always do my best to stay out of jail when investigating.

D and I have a way of negotiating our important and not so important differences with deals. Actually, we make deals on everything. D contends that I fudge the deal whenever I can. Actually, I only do it on the important ones. This one falls into my second tier of deal importance. I figure that if the paper were really important, the police would have found and collected it. The paper intrigues me and my gut feeling is to grab it and to worry about D's response later. Unfortunately for D, it may prove that Tangy is not just the sweet, redheaded customer service goddess who delighted him with great football tickets. This new Tangy delivers more. She may have delivered a brutal death to Todd.

Chapter 3

God, I hate mornings. They should be outlawed. Either that or someone needs to invent an alarm clock that comes attached to a latte machine with a funnel. With all the stupid things advertised on TV, why hasn't someone come up with something useful like that? Based on the fact that I can't smell coffee or hear the cheerful dulcet tones of my man's voice coming from the shower, my guess is that D is still at the police station with Tangy. By my count, that is strike three for her in my justice system. It is amazing what twelve hours can bring. Last night, I went from pampered to peeved to a pounding headache. This morning, I still have the headache and D is still absent. I will have to make my own lattes, which makes my temper go right back over to the extremely pissed side. What a great way to start the day. For two cents, I would just roll back over and spend a few more hours ignoring the world, but then I remember that enticing lead I found last night in Tangy's pink haven.

Three lattes, two aspirins, and a shower later, I can almost see straight again. The question now is how to let D know that I have information about his client without letting him know that I removed evidence from a crime scene. We have this great working relationship, but the straight and narrow lawyer tends to get slightly unbalanced when I do things he considers illegal. Because of that, we have developed our own don't ask, don't tell policy when we work together. Of course, this doesn't follow that I would allow it to be the same in our private lives. What woman would? In that aspect, I follow the tried-and-true method of what he doesn't know, I know is best for our relationship. How could I do anything else as a self-respecting P.I.?

First, I have to get information about this Todd guy. Primarily, I need his full name. I'm good oh, so good in so many ways, but not good enough that I can find someone with just a first name and a possible kinky love of pink. A quick trip to the local police station should take care of that problem. Plus, I will be able to touch base with D and remind him that he has a quality lady at home waiting for his attention and information. It is always good to protect your turf.

D walks into the house as I am leaving. Usually this would be the highlight of my day, but seeing him in his present condition, I'll take a pass at the cute and cuddly that generally occurs. He looks like I feel when the alarm goes off in the morning disheveled, disgruntled, and damned angry. No sleep, no change of clothes, and especially no food don't help his appearance or mood. D is the type of man that takes pride in the way he presents himself professionally. If he is working, then so are his clothes from his tie to his shoes. He is the same when he plays sports-all out and dirty.

"I'm just here for a quick shower, a shave, and a change of clothes. Then I have to get back to the courthouse."

He moves quickly through our cozy house, obviously intent on making this a short visit. I follow just as quickly into the master bedroom suite. I position myself across our bed so I can hear every detail he gives me on this case. I am just as intent on getting all the information I can before he takes off to rescue Tangy again.

"The police are acting like they plan to charge Tangy with murder even though they have no real evidence other than Todd dead outside her door and a record of one previous domestic violence call. I cannot believe they are going to charge her with murder without a witness or weapon, but we all know how these cops in this zip code work. Arrest and charge first so the rich taxpayers think they are being protected."

As D rants on, I figure that this is not the time to bring up the little information I was able to get last night. Who knows maybe that piece of paper was some strange financial pact between Tangy and Todd to start saving a percentage of their wages every month into an IRA and the delivery time was just to remind them when their pizza was arriving. Yeah, right and I can lose twenty pounds overnight by osmosis simply by putting the latest diet book under my pillow.

"D, do you have any further information from Tangy about Todd?" I ask casually as I perch on the bed.

It is a simple question and one that I hope will get D to share a few things without breaking attorney-client privilege. Like the real relationship between Tangy and Todd as well as any information that the police might have disclosed that could simplify my day.

"Yeah," he shouts from the shower. "Todd's last name was Sanchez and he and Tangy have been dating off and on for about a year. They met at a publicity function for the football team. Apparently Todd was a big fan to the point where he would sometimes travel to wherever the team was playing. He was one of those pseudo-sport guys that like to be seen with the owners or sitting behind the bench at the fifty-yard line. Tangy doesn't believe that anyone could dislike Todd enough to want to cause him physical harm and the one call to the police department was when they were first dating and had a loud, but not violent, fight. Baby, that shower felt good. I almost feel human again. How about a kiss and hello now that I look better?"

"You know that you always look perfect to me, babe. I do appreciate you taking a shower before wanting to cuddle me."

"Ah, Rhia. You know that I live solely to please you. Have you had anything to eat yet?"

"No, but I am having a late lunch so all I want is something to tide me over."

"Let me guess you drank a gallon of lattes and nothing else? You know that you need to eat breakfast and not live entirely on caffeine."

"Yes, D. I know. I wasn't hungry and besides, you were not here to prepare something scrumptious for me."

"I can fix that now. Let's move this conversation to the kitchen and see what I can whip up for both of us. I will cook and you will promise to lay off the lattes for the rest of the day. Deal, Rhia?"

"That is a deal!"

As D is cooking up something yummy, I take the chance to once again admire my man. I could look at him all day. I love him so much that I don't know where to begin. His smile can light up a room because it is always genuine. His laugh rocks the couch when he lets it out. His brown eyes sparkle and perfectly complement his hair, which I swear has natural highlights that I would kill to have. Light brown hair with deeper auburn streaks, his hair naturally falls into place. He just comes out of the shower, shakes his head, and then runs his fingers through his hair and he is done. To say that D is built is unnecessary. You can see his guns through his shirts. He played football in college and has retained the athlete's body. I especially love his legs. Strong and straight just like him. His best qualities don't have anything to do with looks. The best part is his sense of humor. It's just like mine. We can be at a party, see something from different areas of the room, look at each other, and then break out laughing. He gets me and I get him. We are *simpatico*.

I head to the living room to turn on the news. D comes out of the kitchen carrying a tray with some tasty variations of our favorite *croque-monsieur*. He added a fried egg to the top of each one. It will be just the perfect mini-meal to get through till a late lunch. Yes, I love D especially when he cooks.

My day is simplified as a result of the information that D shared with me throughout his makeover. Now all I really need to do is to send D off to protect the rights of the innocent and I can get around to finding out what really happened. I hope that it will be a quick trip to the coroner. Standing in the morgue quizzing the medical examiner while he checks the toe tag on some poor slob isn't the best way to start the workday. It is just part of the business. Then it is off for a quick stop at my not-so-plush office and a late lunch just for the hell of it with my closest friends Christy and Carri. If I had a kid and a different profession, I could almost call this a normal day in the life of a soccer mom.

The coroner's office was a dead end. I love coming up with sick puns like that. I think it adds to the smart-ass characterization that people expect of a female P.I. At the coroner's, they were still "processing" the body. That is a polite way to say that they haven't gutted the poor slob yet. I don't know what they have to process. According to Mike, Todd was missing half of his skull. The medical examiner offers to let me watch, but I pass. My guess is that they are hoping to find a remnant of the bullet slug and, if they are really lucky, dope in his system. That would tie everything up nicely for them. Dope cases are always easier to get past a jury. A little insult to a doped-up redhead and, bam, she blows Todd's brains out while he is leaving. Case closed. They may already know how and where Todd died, but they were still in high water with the when, why, and of course the who, as in who shot him, not who was sleeping with him

I like to follow what I call my true path of private investigation procedure. It is time for me to play some football and get into a huddle with my thoughts. I need to go to my office, sit back, and come up with a game plan. Sometimes I like to use the offensive approach. Take the clue and run with it right up the middle and watch people scramble. Then there are the times that I like to play defense and just get some ideas out there and see who comes after me. And there is the old time favorite, I can't figure out where the case is leading, so I punt, wait, and see what yard line I land on.

As I drive across town to the climate-controlled storage center where I have my office, I give Christy and Carri a call to let them know that I might be a few minutes late for our already late lunch. That's one of the great things about these two friends. They will wait for me for hours as long as where we are eating has a liquor license. After one glass of wine, they are only slightly complaining that I am late. After two glasses of wine, they are glad that I will be arriving soon. After three glasses of wine, they no longer care if I even arrive. I may need their help so it is imperative that I get there before they begin the second glass of wine. The stop at the office will have to be short.

I separate my professional life from my personal life by keeping a small, yet dignified establishment. D wants me to move into something more office-like, but a small cubicle at the local storage center serves me very well. I chose an office toward the rear of the complex to give my clients all the privacy I could. Clients can come and go without getting the feeling that someone is watching even though the facility has a twenty-four hour video feed to the main office. I am secure because my office is located in a "secure" facility as their advertising claims. I figure that if people can leave their old furniture and junk here, then I should be just fine. This is the kind of logic that drives D bonkers.

I have a great old desk that I found in a used furniture store. In addition to the desk, which is centered and facing the door, a few shelves lean against one wall, the latest computer sits on the side of the desk, and some framed articles about me that have appeared in local papers hang on the wall. I am ready for business. There are two chairs for clients and under my desk is the most important piece of office equipment. I keep a sawed-off, but heavy, wooden baseball bat handy in case a client or someone I have investigated doesn't like the outcome. Most of the time, I can scare them off with a few swings of the bat and some trash talk about how good I am at hitting all types of balls. Every once in a while, some idiot decides to test how great a hitter I am and generally ends up kissing the floor looking green and moaning. All men should take women at their word. It would make life easier for them. Now that I think about it, I guess my life could never be compared to any soccer mom. They can be fierce on the sidelines, but when I get fierce, I cross all the lines.

I do a quick check of my messages and find out that Tangy has posted bail. A quick call to D and I find out that the owner of the team is taking care of her bond. She is one lucky girl. The ownership of the organization must really want to help her as a show of support and to show how great the organization is or he has another motive. With luck, I will find a reason to get over to the complex to ask a few questions. By "with luck," I mean an opportunity to see my favorite buffed-to-the-end football players up close and personal. I wonder if it is bad taste to ask for their autographs at the same time you are gawking and suggesting that one of their own might be a murderer. I will have to ask Christy for her professional opinion at lunch.

Speaking of lunch, I am now getting dangerously close to the three-drink timeline. I better haul ass if I am to get there in time to enjoy the fun and get their input into the case. Christy is a doctor of psychology. She has spent the last century or so studying the psyche of man. Most people have to pay her big bucks to get her help. She gives it to me free whether I want it or not. In exchange, I keep her up to date on my cases. I like to think that she imagines herself to be me in circumstances as if a beautiful blonde would change places with me in the real world. I bet she'd love to analyze that thought, but I will keep this one to myself. For now, I want her to help me figure out the relationship Tangy had with Todd. I also want to ask her if she thought Tangy was hitting on D with all those free tickets. Carri, her sister, hangs around even through the psych stuff because she hates violence but loves to dish the dirt. Carri has studied some type of therapy for children. She has been a constant source of cases for me. Whenever Carri even suspects that a child is intentionally injured, physically or psychologically, she calls me instead of the police. I do my thing and get the proof whether innocent or guilty and if needed, Carri takes it to social services and the police. This process sometimes gets her in trouble for cutting the red tape, but she doesn't care. She says that she feels the need for speed and helping the kids is all that matters.

Going anywhere with Christy and Carri is always an experience. I have gotten in more trouble when I am with them than I do anywhere else with the exception of work. Christy and Carri are identical twins. Blonde, tall, slim, gorgeous twins who capture the attention of every male in the room. Now I'm no slouch in the looks department. I have long brown hair that stays under control most of the time. I try to stay fit and watch what I eat except during stakeouts. I have great, deep silver-blue eyes and I know how to act like a lady when I have to compliments of my mother. Put me next to Christy and Carri and I become invisible. I become the third seat that men ask whether it is available even when I am sitting on it. I once heard of an interesting social experiment. A guy I knew in college claimed that every group of girls makes sure that at least one of the girls in the group is ugly. He claimed that this girl was usually the smart one. Her purpose in the group was to tutor the other girls while also making them look more attractive by comparison. What a sexist pig he was!

If this is true, then I would fit the bill as the ugly friend because compared to the Christy-Carri combo, I don't get noticed that much. That is until D came around. I told you he was highly intelligent.

"Where are my babes?" I shout as I enter our current favorite joint. Christy and Carri both love some show about a guy with spiked hair who travels around eating in places that tourists avoid. That is how we found "The Hole" currently our favorite spot to eat, drink, and be loud. It is hidden behind a gas station. Wait let me rephrase that. Technically it is part food spot and gas station. Let's just say that when you eat or drink at The Hole, you can get your car tuned up at the same time. Nothing fancy here just great sandwiches, salads, and lots of American beer on tap and Mexican beer in bottles served with limes. Carri really likes the place because everything they fix is supposedly organic and free range. Whatever that means is beyond me, but is important to her. She is currently on a super health kick. I think her health kick has something to do with the new man in her life. She is exercising with him as he gets ready for some sort of fitness test. She promises to tell me more about her new man later. I agree reluctantly to wait. I just hope that this guy is better than the last one, but he is a subject Carri doesn't want to revisit and I agree. I have more important details on which to focus. Tonight I need The Hole to be the perfect place to gather my thoughts with the help of my friends and possibly plan for a crazy stakeout night.

"Murder is not the crime of the criminals, but that of law-abiding citizens."

Emmanuel Teney

Chapter 4

Tonight is stakeout night. Normally I am a top-down, radio-full-on, cruise-in-my-Corvette kind of gal. Stakeouts require something a little more toned down. Fortunately, I am an old car junkie. I never trade in a car. Instead, I add it to what I call my stable of has-beens. First, there is beat up Big Bertha, my lady who does the hard haulin' work and the one I drive when I want to be one of the guys. Then, there is the sleek 'Vette that I call Black Velvet, the gal I drive when I need to be noticed and appreciated by anyone I am lucky to pass. Finally an old sedan named Fiona. She fills the need for a no-notice type of transportation. Unfortunately, Fiona, the subcompact American-made gray sedan, is not the one I choose when I want comfort. It is one of the many reasons that I hate this part of investigative work. Add hours of boredom and constant snacking on things I've given up for my perpetual Lent and this becomes my absolute least favorite of all my least favorite things to do on a case. Luckily, Christy is available to ride along with me tonight.

Christy makes a great partner in crime on stakeout nights such as tonight. Her quick wit can keep me awake and laughing for hours. Plus, she has an unbelievable ability to stay awake through long night hours due to copious amounts of caffeine-laced drinks. I won't have to break the no-more-lattes deal I made with D earlier. Having Christy as a partner tonight means I can get in a power nap if I need a quick timeout after this long, annoying day. Carri rarely tags along. She is more of the early-to-bed, early-to-rise kind, which leaves Christy and me time to talk about Carri and her new beau and his unusual name. Con, or Constant as he is legally called, is joining our tight circle. D and Ben, D's best friend, took to Con immediately. No questions asked no need to think about how he fits into the group. Just hi, want to play poker and watch the game and all the guys are best buds. Sometimes I can't understand how men think. Tonight will give Christy and me time to decide if Con gets to stay and if we will let him have our Carri.

"Christy, tell me all you can about Con."

"You will probably be able to get as much information from D, Rhia. He has spent more time with him. I have only spent a few minutes with him when he picks Carri up for their dates. Con is really quiet when you first meet. He is easy on the eyes with dark almost black short hair. He's an officer in the army. That is all Carri has shared with me. She is keeping this one all to herself. Did you know that she called D and asked him to include Con in another poker game?"

"Carri probably wants D's help to get Con nice and comfortable with the guys before she unleashes you and me on him. Maybe she thinks we will scare him off between the background check and the psychoanalyzing."

"If my sister thinks the two of us can scare off a man, she shouldn't be dating him. I will give her one more date and if she doesn't give me the full information briefing, she will be in big trouble. I will say that Carri is usually very talkative and divulges all the information to me when she meets a new guy. This is different, which makes me think she is falling fast. One week more and she better set up an evening where we can all get a shot at interrogating Con or else!"

We arrive on Tangy's street and I choose a quiet parking

spot down from the condo. Once we are sitting pretty and as comfortable as we can in the limited space of a subcompact, I bring Christy up to speed on this case.

"Tangy has D tied up in knots," I explain. "D thinks she can do no wrong since she works for the football team and occasionally gets him free tickets. I think she will hit on anything male that passes by, and maybe she hit on the wrong one when she got mixed up with Todd. I made a few calls this afternoon while at the office and found out that Todd had some deep gambling debts hanging over his head."

"Maybe he hooked up with Tangy hoping to get inside information on the team to help him decide how to place his next bets to get out of trouble."

"That seems like a lot of trouble to go through just to get information about the team. Couldn't he get all the information he wanted on the Internet and forget having to deal with some girl," replied Christy.

"Well, from what I have gathered about Todd's betting, he doesn't come across as the brightest of men and I keep forgetting that you haven't met or had the pleasure of talking with Tangy. Between the red hair, long legs, and the sweet little-girl voice, I think she could sell anything to any male around. Every time Tangy would comp free tickets to D, he would come home with a glazed look in his eyes."

"Now I know that you are exaggerating, Rhia. D would never look at another woman. He is totally in love with you."

"I know but that doesn't mean he can't appreciate a great-looking woman when he sees one and I get the feeling Tangy is a type that likes to be appreciated by all men all the time. And please, don't use the 'in love' term. I prefer that D just be totally in lust with me. Every time the conversation includes the word love, I see myself surrounded by picket fences, four cats, a couple of dogs, guinea pigs, and twelve kids."

Laughing, Christy replies, "Shall we talk about your major

commitment issues now? Do you need to visit my office on a professional basis?"

"No, thank you. Want to talk about all the guys you date and why you haven't found the perfect one yet? I think you can match me on the commitment issues."

"Touché. You win this round, Rhia. I've had a relatively easy day with my patients and got sleep last night so why don't you get one of your famous power naps and I will wake you if a redhead leaves the condo building. But please, no snoring!"

"Thanks. Contrary to what D says, I don't snore! Remember what Mother says ladies don't snore, they just breathe heavily."

"Rhia, just go to sleep while you have the chance."

My brain is telling me it was just moments, but it is several hours later when Christy wakes me up and tells me it is time to go into P.I. action. A redhead walked out of the condo building, glanced around, and then entered the garage. One would have thought that a night at the police station answering questions, followed by a day getting arraigned in court and dealing with a bail bondsman not to mention explaining it all to your boss would have tired Tangy to the point that she would want to remain at home. But when a woman has something on her mind, she has to go the distance. Apparently Tangy still has some distance to go, because just as I am wiping the sleep out of my eyes and quickly trying to down some not-so-hot coffee in spite of the deal I made with D, Tangy pulls out of the condo garage in a sleek apple-red roadster like she had just heard of a designer 75-percent-off shoe sale.

Chapter 5

Tailing Tangy is easy. She is so easy to follow that it is insulting to my skills. Hey, I am a pro. I take pride in my work and here we are tooling along without a care. Not only do I not have to use my best tailing techniques, I don't have to use any technique. She hasn't looked in the rearview mirror once.

"I don't think D has told Tangy that I am on the job yet. Or else she totally underestimates me and my quest for the truth because she is definitely in her own world right now. Not to mention she is one hell of a hurry. What's your take, Christy?"

"Actually, I was thinking she isn't D's type so I am trying to figure out why you have such a problem with her."

"It's my nature. You're a person who looks at the way people think and try to help them. I think everyone is out to screw me somehow so I am always looking to outthink them first especially if D is involved and the other person is female."

"I swear you crack me up, Rhia. You have a unique view of the world and I think down the road, we are going to have to discuss this professionally. You know I will be happy to give you a discount."

"Why, Christy? What a generous offer, but I will pass. If you start trying to figure out all of my idiosyncrasies, you won't have time for your other patients."

"Don't forget, Rhia, we can also talk about your wonderful mother and how she drives you bonkers with wedding talk."

"I am glad that you made that last statement laughing. Really, Christy! Bonkers? Is that a professional term? Maybe we should discuss both of our mothers. Now that they are the best of friends, we will probably spend every waking hour trying to figure out what they have planned for us."

"Rhia, now that you bring up the friendship, I'm hoping they will be so busy with each other that it will keep them out of our love lives for awhile."

"We can only hope, Christy. If it doesn't, let's encourage them to spend time with Carri and Con!"

"Rhia, you have a mean streak, but that is a great, yet deviant, idea. I like it immensely."

"Look, Christy. Tangy is turning. This direction can only mean one thing. Tangy is going from the upscale side of town to the top of the town. The people who live here are more than the movers and shakers. They are the people who own the companies that motivate the movers and shakers."

Just as I finish the sentence, Tangy made a hard right and I knew exactly where she was headed. Tailing her just got tantalizing. Tangy is heading to a man's house. This block has only three houses and one of the dwellings belongs to none other than the man who put up the money for her bail.

"Well, Christy, look what we have here. It seems a strange time of night to stop by to say thanks for bailing me out of jail. What or should I say who could have Tangy so worked up that she has to speed over here at this hour. This makes me believe that there is more between the boss man and our girl, Tangy. Stockman put up the bail bond for her. I wonder if he is her sugar daddy on a regular basis. I may have to do an in-depth check of her finances. See if I can connect some dots between the two of them financially. This could also be a love triangle gone wrong."

"Rhia, I will say this about you. You sure know how to show a girl a good time. I may even get a professional paper out of this evening. How stress and death can cause strange bedfellows. I like that as a title. I can discuss the psychological reasons certain people bond over bail money."

"Christy, I think you humor may be as warped as mine."

"Why thank you, Rhia. Knowing your humor as I do, I take that as a compliment. Didn't this guy just become single again after his latest divorce?"

"I don't do divorces, too messy, but even I know that he is available. You couldn't pick up a paper in this town without reading something about the mess."

"Psychologically speaking, I think this Tangy has a whole lot more to her than we think."

"My guess is that Tangy is going to be here for the rest of the night. It's time to go home, wake up D, and let him know that I think Tangy may be slightly shady if not completely dishonest. Poor D, first he gets a murder and now he may lose his contact for free football tickets if Tangy turns out to be less victim than perp."

After dropping off Christy at the expensive townhouse she shares with Carri, I head home to what I hope is a warm bed and a hot hunk. Although it has been a long day and two long nights, my brain is going a mile a minute. Questions are flying through my mind without time enough for me to come up with logical answers. Why was Tangy heading over to the owner of the team's house in the middle of the night? Why was the owner of the team even involved? Normally these types avoid negative publicity especially when it involves the team personnel and may adversely affect ticket sales. What relationship did Tangy really have with the rich, newly divorced guy? For that matter, what was the relationship between Tangy and Todd? Was there some strange threesome thing going on in the wealthy suburb? God, I hope not. I hate those cases. Anything dealing with complicated domestic bliss always ends badly. But then things had already ended badly for Todd. As tired as I am, the real and only question is whether I wake up D and let him have some bad news or just spoon in and wait for the dawn.

I pull up to the house and realize that spooning is not an option. The lights are all on and the guys' cars are still in the drive. The poker game must be hot tonight. At least that is what I thought until I enter our house and find the guys bunched around the television with D who has a miserable look on his face. Guess he's received the bad news about Tangy before I even got home.

"Hey guys, what is the excitement on the TV?"

"I wouldn't exactly call it excitement," answers Ben.

I acknowledge Ben and glance at D. To say that he looks miserable is an understatement. I haven't seen him look this lousy since he had the stomach flu on the same day that he lost his shirt betting on the Final Four. Some unknown TV journalist is yakking on about breaking news on our very own murder case. Seems Christy and I weren't the only ones on a stakeout tonight. Someone has just leaked the news that our very own Tangy had a late night rendezvous with her very own version of Little Orphan Annie's Daddy Warbucks. My initial guess is that a friend of a friend of one of his ex-wives decided to do a little payback. The problem for me is that D will be paying the price. His murder case just got complicated and we all know I hate complications in my life. He is now the lawyer of record for what the media has dubbed "Fourth Down and Murder."

Chapter 6

This morning was a three-aspirin morning just to get out of bed. After last night and the blow up on the news about Tangy stepping out at midnight to catch up on ticket sales with her boss at his new bachelor pad, D decided to go into his office later than usual. We both know that to get to his office today, he is going to have to lower his shoulders, charge forward, break some tackles and get to the end zone, the front door, as quickly as possible. A phone call earlier alerted D to the fact that it seemed every journalist and photographer was camped out waiting for his arrival. I tried to cheer him up by reminding him that this was great publicity for his law firm. Unfortunately, that didn't fly. Not when the case you are on has just received the catchy title "Fourth Down and Murder."

D's day got even more unpleasant when I started to give him the information I had on Todd and his gambling debts. I tried to sugarcoat the information I found on the piece of paper in Tangy's condo, but halfway through the conversation D stopped, looked at me with suspicion , and asked where I had acquired the information. Busted! Try as I might, I could not get D off the fact that I had removed evidence from a crime scene.

"Rhia, the key word is *look around*. Not take apart furniture and sneak evidence out of the apartment even if Mike was at the scene. I bet he wasn't even in the apartment when you were in there snooping."

"For your information, I do not snoop. Amateurs snoop. I investigate and don't you forget it, buddy. Besides, I didn't take anything from Tangy's apartment. I took it from her condo."

"Nice touch with the condo correction, Rhia, but you could really be in deep trouble with the police."

"D, can you take a break from being my lawyer and become my chef extraordinaire? I could use something to eat. Do you think you could make us a nice brunch? I really need caffeine, sugar, and starch if you want to continue this conversation."

"Rhia, only you can convince me to stop giving legal advice in favor of cooking. It is that look you give me. I fall for it every time and you know it. I think I will add some protein to your request. How do savory crepes and lattes sound?"

"Yummy! You cook and I'll talk. By the time you have finished preparing our feast, I will have you totally convinced that my actions have all been above board."

"I doubt that, but talk away."

"I intend to let the police have this information just as soon as I am through with it. I just wanted a little time to figure out what it had to do with Todd and Tangy. Then I have to find out what the figure 1.5 million means and finally discover what is going to be delivered at a very specific time and place. Not to mention who is making the delivery and who will be accepting the delivery and did the number 1.5 million mean 1.5 million dollars. Is it payment for services? Simple stuff if it wasn't for the fact that one of the people named on the paper will not be able to go anywhere without a posse of news people and paparazzi. The other is just plain out of commission. Todd is dead. D, I hate to say this, but you need to go see Tangy and get her talking. I don't care if it takes all day. She is deep into this situation and if she wants to stay out of jail, it is time for her to give you the truth-the *complete* truth."

I pause and wait for D to digest all the information. I still know that we have one more item on our agenda.

"Really Rhia that is all you have to figure out before you turn over the illegally obtained evidence to the police?"

"Just to make you happy, I am going by the police station right after we finish eating and imply that I found this somewhere around the condo when Mike let me in to have a quick look. I will tell them that it didn't strike me as all that valuable until I saw the news today. As a good citizen, I knew that I had to immediately come in and disclose this info and give them the paper. I will say I couldn't do it earlier because I was with my psychologist for several hours discussing something extremely important and very personal. That should work and I was with Christy so it is not really lying."

Sarcastically D responds, "Call me when they arrest you. I know the station well and will try to negotiate the best cell for you. Let's eat now. It may be your last good meal for awhile."

Poor D sometimes I wonder if he has any faith in me. All I have to do is run into good old Mike and hand the paper to him and he will cover for me. I hope that I will be able to scope out some additional information if I hang around the station. This case has too many twists too early in the investigation and I need to start separating the strings so I can get to the best line of thought and action. Right now, the case is tied up with possibilities and no solutions. That doesn't help D defend Tangy not that I care that much about Tangy but I do care about D and his reputation as a lawyer. I need to solve this so D can win his case or if she is guilty like I am beginning to think she is, do some pretty major plea bargaining. I want proper justice to happen, but more than that, I want D okay at the end of this. If Tangy ends up hurting D in any way, well, Tangy and I are going to dance jail or no jail. I need to go back to work pronto. I give D a kiss good-bye and a promise to be good and head out the door.

The police station is filled with reporters. I did not know that we had so many in this little independent, upscale suburb tucked neatly inside San Antonio. I wonder if reporters have the capability to clone themselves when a big, juicy story surfaces. These guys and girls all look the same. Constantly touching up makeup and hair and asking their photographers how they look. What a strange time we live in when news reporters have a larger posse than the person making the news. After this case, I am taking a vacation to someplace where there is no radio, no papers, and no TV.

The good thing about all this commotion is that the police are so busy trying to keep order that I should be able to drop off this evidence and not land in jail. I see Mike hanging back by his desk. As usual, he is eating something unhealthy.

"Hi, Mike. I came by today because I forgot to give something to you when I left the condo the other night."

"Really? You just forgot? You didn't accidentally put what I am sure is evidence, somewhere out of sight so I wouldn't tell you to leave it and get out."

"Now, Mike. You know me and how I am always on your side. I would never try to pull one over on an old-school cop like you. You are too quick at police work and so much more astute than the others at this station."

"Okay already, you can lay off the bullshit and just give it to me now. I won't let them know that you took it. I'd hate to have to lock you up or have you lose your P.I. license, but you owe me."

"Here you go. Name the favor, Mike, and it will be taken care of as soon as this case is finished."

"Make it sooner my oldest daughter is dating a scumbag and I want a full workup on him. That is the payback and I want every stone uncovered where this guy is concerned. I've promised her that I won't do anything to scare this one off, but I still think I need more information before my little girl gets too attached."

"Wow, you must really love this guy, Mike. I promise to get right on it when I am done with D's case today. Until then, keep safe and start eating the low-cal bagels. It looks like you are putting on a little weight, Mike."

"Rhia, time to leave before I change my mind and book you for obstruction."

Too many people are hanging around the police station so I decide to swing by my office, check the mail, and do a little housekeeping on the computer and then some major digging in the ether of the computer world to find information on the one and only owner of our local pro football team. Imagine my surprise when I view a very dark, very luxurious, long black sedan parked at my office door with a chauffeur standing by the back of the car just waiting to open the door and let the occupant grace my professional abode. As I park my car, out steps one of the players in our little story. I get my first up close and personal look at one of the wealthiest and most eligible bachelors of our area. The one-and-only Silence Sterling Stockman is at my door. Now what does the owner of the pro football team want with little old me? Obviously he already has Tangy, and I am one girl who never would lower herself for sloppy seconds.

"Behind every great fortune is a crime."

Honore de Balzac

Chapter 7

Silence is anything but silent. I feel as if I am at a cocktail party for the socially challenged as he walks around my office like a cat on the prowl. His non-stop talking does give me time to observe this godsend to the female population. How four women got infatuated with this Romeo is beyond me. His antics on the sidelines of the football field make the sport talk shows constantly. His mouth gets him into trouble all the time. The league fines him on a regular basis. He isn't exactly what I would call handsome. He is no D. His hair is slicked. It actually shines from all of the hair product he uses. His face is long with eyes that are too close for my taste. For a forty-plus-year-old-man, the muscles in his face don't move as they should while he is talking. My guess is that he has had numerous trips to a face doc to get Botox. How can good-looking women find vain men attractive? Must be the money or maybe it is the close proximity you can get to the football players if you are married to him. I seem to recall that his second wife found a warm refuge with one of the lineman. It was quite a deal back then with both parties player and wife getting released to other teams. It was probably the only divorce that didn't cost him plenty.

I wish Christy were here right now. She would have a field

day with this one. First, there is the odd name Silence. Guess one of his parents was a Benjamin Franklin fan. Either that or they really didn't want a kid. I want to break his conversation with himself to ask him if he got beaten up on the playground because of his name, but I am mesmerized by his actions. One would think that he is in front of a camera giving an interview instead of a little P.I. office in a climate-controlled storage center.

Silence is smooth. I have to give him that. He talks fast and flashes lots of jewelry with large stones. The longer I look at him, the less I understand his appeal to women. No six-pack hiding under his shirt and, while his style may be expensive, it is way too trendy for me. He wants to dominate the conversation from the beginning. Hell, I don't think he has taken a breath since he entered the office. He is on a mission and it is time for me to find out exactly what he really wants.

"Mr. Stockman, please have a seat. Obviously, there is something important that you wish to discuss with me if you came all the way down here to my office without an appointment."

I am so intuitive sometimes that I astound myself. It probably sounded sarcastic, but, hell, the man just showed up here as if I would be waiting and didn't have anything better to do. Of course, it makes my job easier because I doubt I could get past his staff or security if I showed up unannounced at his door but that is beside the point. I am not intimidated easily. My ego is too big for that and I want good old Silence to realize that from the beginning.

"Mrs. O'Neil, I wish to hire you to look into the death of Todd Sanchez. An associate of mine has been charged with this heinous crime. I want her cleared as quickly as possible."

"Mrs. O'Neil is my mother, Mr. Stockman. You can call me Rhia. and I am already looking into the case for another client."

I lean forward in a move that should show Stockman that I am not impressed or intimidated by his demeanor or money.

"Really? Who? I am glad that someone is taking Tangy's

innocence seriously. I will pay you handsomely to keep me in the loop concerning any information that you acquire."

"Unfortunately, Mr. Stockman, I can't accommodate you. I don't share information unless I have the approval of the other client and I have the notion that the client would prefer that I keep all information confidential."

What I really want to say is that I never "in-the-loop" with a man on a first meet-and-greet, but I doubted he would appreciate my wit right now. I also don't want to annoy him just yet. I need more information first.

"Mr. Stockman, I assume that you are close to Tangy and that is why you are here today. Has Tangy worked closely with you for long?"

I hope if I emphasize closely enough, he will relax a bit and slip up, but you don't get to be as rich as he is by being stupid.

"Actually, I don't work closely with Tangy at all. In fact, I barely know her. I am really here to protect my team. Tangy is in ticket sales and works in just one aspect of the total team project. I assure you that my interest is really for the benefit of all the investors and players. Bad publicity is not good for business. Plus, my staff has briefed me that Tangy could not do anything as vile as murder. From everything I have heard, this is a gross miscarriage of justice and we need to do all we can to see it is rectified as quickly as possible."

I keep a polite smile on my face, but I am fuming inside. Who do you think you are fooling, buddy? Bling and manners won't seal this deal. I want to reach across the desk and dope-slap him upside his head while asking him what Tangy was doing at his house late last night. Hi, boss. Just stopped by to give you an update on ticket sales, my ass. Now is not the time to reveal my game plan. Something is going on between Todd, Tangy, and Mr. Stockman. The more he talks, the more I realize that Silence is sleazy and possibly criminal. I will have to find out how sleazy and how much of a criminal he is.

"Mr. Stockman, I have to cut this meeting short. I have

another appointment across town. I will do everything I can to alleviate any bad publicity for you and your football team. I am a huge fan. Would it be possible for me to stop by your office at the sports facility should I need additional information concerning Tangy?"

Being nice to a jerk is an effort, but I have my mother's voice in my head saying something about bees, vinegar, and honey, so I keep laying it thickly.

"It has been such a pleasure meeting you and Tangy is so lucky to have an employer who takes her welfare so seriously. I will contact my other client and seek permission to share all information with you."

Believe this and I have some swampland to sell to you. I have to admit that Silence is holding his cards close to his chest because I can't tell immediately if my nice approach is working. The usual pleasantries are exchanged and Silence leaves with the chauffeur heavily hitting the gas. My guess is that Silence isn't too happy with the meeting or with me. I really don't care. As I have said before, nice isn't really my thing but I did get one opportunity of value out of the conversation. I can now stop by the sports complex any time and ask as many questions as I want all with the permission of the boss man. I guess Silence really is golden.

Chapter 8

I need a bath. A long, hot, deep bath with lots of smelly lavender bubbles is what I desire tonight. I had a brief telephone call with my beloved D, but he didn't go into details while in a crowded police station. Apparently, the police have new evidence and want to ask Tangy more questions. I know that this has become a high-profile murder with a new catchy name thanks to the news hawkers, but I want D home tonight. We need to touch base face-to-face, body-to-body. It has been too long since I have had that man's arms around me. I want to know, at least for one night, that I am the only woman that he is thinking about and the only woman he wants. I know he will have questions about what I have uncovered, while I want to know if Tangy has finally opened up with dirt for D or if she was still posing as the poor, helpless victim. That is why I want to know everything, but not tonight. My need is great for a long bath, one of my favorite drinks, and then D waiting for me. If he wants to free his mind of all the recent turmoil by whipping up something decadent, then I will not complain about that type of delay. I am officially freeing up tonight for us and only us. It is to be a rocking night that leaves both of us sated and wishing for a repeat even when we know we have to reenter the real world when it is over.

As the bubbles start filling up our oversized tub, I go to make myself a calming drink. What kind of drink is right for tonight? Would a nice pinot grigio do or should I go for something stronger? I can always make one of my famous Eastern Shore Pink Lemonades, but that seems too summery for football weather. For a cool fall night, I think I will go with something more appropriate such as a Snuggler, French Tea, or Tea Au Vin. After some thought about the day and my current brain function, I opt for the Tea Au Vin. It is the best combination of everything I need a hot smooth drink with a soothing kick.

I place the red wine into the cup and microwave it until it is nice and hot. Then I let the teabag float in the wine for a few minutes and perfection occurs. I first had this drink at a small café in Verbier, Switzerland. D and I were there for a weeklong ski vacation. D is an expert skier. It is exciting to watch him gracefully blast down the black diamond slopes with his powerful strength. Plus, he looks so great in his ski outfit. Sipping the mellow drink and sitting in the bubbles is definitely calming. I light a few candles to help set the mood and let my softer side come out for once. D says that I should let the softer side come out more often, but that is just not who I am most of the time. D has also said that I let my softer side come out when I want to get him to do something he doesn't want to do. It's true that I can play the game that way, but I don't try to manipulate D. I have too much respect and love for him. I can get just as much out of him by winning at baseball on the games we play on our computer.

"Hello, Rhia! Are you home?" D bellows as he enters our home.

"D, I am in the bathroom."

He enters, glances at all the bubbles, and says, "I guess you had an interesting day. Let me get out of these clothes. No baby, don't get up. Stay where you are and I will join you even if I end up smelling likes some flowers. Deal?"

"Deal. Welcome home, babe. I am glad that you got home this early. I was afraid you would be gone for hours."

D eases into the water, pushing all the bubbles to my side.

"Well, my darling P.I., want to talk shop?"

"Sure, D. For awhile anyway then I would like to move on to not talking unless it is pillow talk. Deal?"

"Deal."

"D, what did the police tell you when you were at the station with Tangy the last time? What questions did they ask Tangy? How did she answer the questions? Did she mention Mr. Silence Sterling Stockman? What about Todd Sanchez? Is there any more information on him or if he might be connected to Mr. Stockman? Was anyone after Todd because of his gambling debts? And did the police happen to mention anything about 1.5 million of something and any strange deliveries that might have occurred in the last twenty-four hours? Has the coroner released his report yet?"

"Obviously, the warmth of the bath hasn't calmed you down. Are you done, Rhia, so I can get a word in to the conversation?"

"Yeah, but before you begin, I got a visit at my office from the man himself, Mr. Silence Sterling Stockman."

"Why didn't you call me to come over? I don't like it when you have office meetings with men in that dump you call an office."

"Chill babe, I can handle myself. Besides, my office is secure via videocam to the main office. You know that so there is no reason to freak. Maybe you're just jealous because the newly free, ultra-rich bachelor stopped by my little abode to converse with sweet and sexy me."

"I swear, Rhia, he touches you once in any way and he is going to find himself in major legal trouble in every way I can find to make his life miserable."

"Ah, my love, my dearest D, I love it when you talk legal dirty!"

I get a smirk for that comment and a few minutes later D

suggests that we leave our oversized tub. I am not ready. It is nice to be close to him and spend a few minutes in quiet, just chilling. I keep adding hot water so we can stay longer, but eventually the candles are low and the bubbles are gone. We use the last few moments to take a time out from talking and just enjoy the quiet and our drinks. This all-too-brief interlude was wonderful and neither of us wants to let it end. Eventually D leaves and heads to the kitchen and fixes two more Tea Au Vins and we meet at the entrance to the bedroom.

"D, let's forget everything tonight. I am so relaxed that I don't care what is going on in the outside world. Can we make a deal to let everything go but each other?"

"Deal and might I add it was a very easy deal to make with my beautiful better half. I am wasted from all the stress of the last few days."

"Stressed? I think I know just how to de-stress my man. By the time I am done, you won't even remember your name let alone the case. Deal?"

"Deal! That is most definitely a deal."

The lights are off and my night begins with a sweet, soft sigh.

Chapter 9

What a difference a well-earned night of frolicking and sleep can do for a girl. I actually got out of bed the first time D called from the kitchen to tell me he was starting my latte. I grabbed a quick shower, joined D in the kitchen, and downed latte number one. I even talked D into making a second latte and didn't get his usual lecture on caffeine. The hot shower, the lattes, and D's smile might actually make me start liking mornings. D offers to make us a great breakfast, but I tell him I am meeting the twins for an early lunch so I will just have lattes. Instead of cooking, he spends the time bringing me up to date on the latest news from the police. The coroner finally released his preliminary report. Todd Sanchez was shot with a .45 at very close range. The gun has not been found. The slug markings are not in the system. Police records of other crimes indicate that this gun has not been used before in any crimes. Lucky Todd. The bullet that blew his brains out was a virgin.

This case is getting more complicated as time passes. It shouldn't be complicated. There are not that many players involved. It is frustrating because I can't seem to get a handle on it. I'm really starting to get royally pissed off at the case and myself. It is time to get serious and to find out who did what to whom and why. Tangy is not cooperating or she is smarter that I first thought. Maybe she has heard the statistic that most criminals convict themselves because they won't keep their mouths shut. I didn't take her for someone who would keep quiet. Of course, she may actually be innocent, but that is something I really doubt. Not that I am influenced by my initial and unjustified jealousy toward the girl.

The early morning with D was great, but I need to get my derriere in gear. I have just enough time to swing by my office and hit the computer for some research before I meet my girls at The Hole. I have plenty of people to research, but what I can't figure out is the 1.5 million number. The most natural thing to assume is that it means millions of dollars, but any good P.I. will tell you never to assume anything. There is a connection here between the three suspects besides the usual "we all love our football team" aspect. I need to find out what that connection is and soon. I am talking with Christy on the cell when I pull around the storage complex. As I pull into my office parking lot, I immediately get the feeling that everything is not kosher. It could be the parked police car or the fact that the manager of the facility is standing outside my door. He is with several members of our very own police force. I tell Christy that the police are outside my office and I will call her back as soon as I know what is happening.

"Hi guys. Is something going on or are you all here to make my morning even better?" I ask as I am getting out of Black Velvet.

I know immediately that they are just waiting for me. That is simple to deduce once I get a quick glance at the door to my office. Someone has left the door ajar, which would be easy since the doorjamb looks like a sledgehammer had a field day with it. There goes my security deposit! Will this be covered by insurance? I know I have more serious issues than those. I have some pretty confidential stuff on my computer. If someone has copied my stuff and can figure out my crazy code and decipher it, I could be screwed as well as in trouble with some previous clients. I give a quick text to Christy and Carri to let them know that I will have to change our meet at The Hole from a late breakfast to a late lunch. After several more texts to assure them that I am okay, I can give my full attention to the anxious manager and the police.

"It looks like a simple smash and grab, ma'am " says the younger of the two policemen.

Now my day is really ruined. Junior officer just called me "ma'am." I know that he is just being police polite, but you don't call a woman of my age "ma'am" unless you want to get slapped. I'm not over the hill, but it has been a few years since I saw my twenties. "Ma'am" automatically brings up conversations with my mother over my biological clock and her strong desire for grandchildren.

The building manager, knowing my temper extremely well from some previous issues over other nearby occupants, and loud, bad music, quickly cuts in and lets me know that the interior is fine.

"It doesn't look like they even entered your office. The alarm went off as soon as they breached the door and triggered an automatic call to the police. The alarm company also called me and I viewed the feed and came down immediately. I've given the tape to the police, but it doesn't show a good picture of the intruder. He had a hat pulled low over his face and parked his car in such a way that you can't see the license plate."

The facility has twenty-four hour feed to the main office, but that doesn't mean that someone sits in the office twenty-four hours. Not at the prices they charge. I enter the office to check for damage. The inside of my office looked just as I left it the last time I was here.

One of the police officers behind me asks, "Is there anyone who would want to do you harm or steal anything of unusual value that you might store in the office?"

I answer, "Not that I can think of at this time. Most of my current cases are pretty tame in nature."

I choose not to disclose to the police that the case I am investigating now is their very own "Fourth Down and Murder." I can't see any benefit in dragging this out and I really want private time to hit my computer and check the contents just to verify that no one has touched it. After a few more minutes signing papers and assuring the police that I will contact them if I find anything missing, they take off. Once I am sure that a new door will be installed immediately and that I will not be charged, I act as if I am relieved. The manager of the complex is intent on assuring me that, since it was a malicious act from an unknown person, the facility insurance will cover damages. All I want is for him to leave. I finally get rid of the building manager. Now I can get to the real issue. Who is so scared of what I haven't uncovered that they would risk breaking into my office?

I need to think and fast. D is going to go ballistic when he finds out that my office has been targeted for destruction. When he gets upset over my work and safety, walls are not safe. That man can put a hole in the wall so fast that my head spins. Then, we will have to have the usual you-don't-have-to-work-at-something-dangerous-I-can-take-care-of-you conversation again. Chances are that I won't be able to keep this quiet since the twins already know, which means Ben knows, which means D already knows. He probably hasn't called yet because he is in court and has turned off his phone. I know that call is coming. I hope that no one thought to call or text my mother. Time to seriously think of how to calm D down so he doesn't fire me from the case for my own good. I'm not giving up this case not after some creep knocked down my door.

Just as I am coming up with a plausible defense to give to my lawyer, the phone rings. I don't have to check the caller ID to know that it is D. I can feel the anger through the ring. "D, I'm okay. Everything is fine. Please don't freak out. The current plans are for me to head to The Hole for a late lunch with Christy and Carri. After that, I will work at home. I can access my computer for e-mails from our computer and I promise not to get into any more trouble before you get home from work."

"Rhia, if I knew that you might get hurt or someone would break into your office when I took that phone call from Tangy, I would have let the phone ring till eternity. I am so sorry. Are you sure you are all right? What if you had been there when they tried to break into the place? You know how I feel about you and your work?"

"Yes, babe, I know. I told you how much I loved my work when you got involved with me. Remember that it was a total package deal or no deal at all. I promise everything is fine and this may not have anything to do with Tangy's case. It may just be someone who knew I have a new computer in the office and wanted to grab some extra black market cash."

I figure D doesn't have to know that the person who destroyed my door knew how to avoid the security camera. Better to let him believe that it was some lowlife that needed some easy cash.

"Still, Rhia, when are you leaving to meet Christy and Carri?"

"D, I will text them as soon as we get off the phone. I'll find out if we can still meet for a late lunch and then head over to The Hole. I am going to spend the rest of the afternoon chilling out with our friends. If they can't break for lunch this late, then I promise to head straight home. Is it a deal?"

"Deal, but don't fudge anything on this deal, Rhia! I want to know that when I hang up, I can go back to work and know that you are safe."

With that last comment he signs off.

Now that I had calmed down D, I can get back to work. I feel bad that I am misleading D, but I justify it to myself that it is in his best interest. He needs to concentrate on his court cases and clients other than Tangy. I have to figure out a way to get around the latest deal with D so he doesn't get mad at me later. Wow, that man can get protective fast. I'll keep to the deal as much as I can, but I have no intention of giving up on this case. This wasn't a break-in for cash. Someone has targeted my office and that makes me a target. When I want someone's eyes on me, it is because I am in the mood to be noticed. I want to let whatever creep thought he could scare me off know that I am not scared. It will take more than a smashed door to move me to back off. They better watch out. I'm really motivated now.

Chapter 10

Lunch at The Hole with Christy and Carrie is just what I need. Between the two of them, they temporarily take my mind off the case, D's unnecessary concern, and the total destruction of my office door. Sometimes a quick break from confusing evidence is just what a good private investigator needs. Unfortunately, there have been too many breaks in this case and none of them have been good. Now is not the time to start over-thinking the situation. That can confuse a case faster than bogus evidence. If this thing doesn't start taking fewer twists and turns to nowhere, I may have to think seriously about a new career. I know I will have to go through the I-promise-I-am-okay routine again for the benefit of the twins. I hope that they will arrive at the same time and I will only have to do it once. After that, we can get on to the really important issues such as wine and our guys.

I really want to get Carri's input on Constant. Suddenly, there seem to be new men in my life with unusual first names: first Constant and now Silence. What I really want to know is whether Carri and Christy think this guy will live up to his name. The last jerk Carri dated was anything but constant. The fact that my suspicions and subsequent investigation proved the point still bothers me. Normally, I stay out of friends' private lives unless invited to look into something, but I am territorial where Christy and Carri are concerned. To me, they are sisters in fact, they're closer than sisters are, if that is possible. I don't like anyone to mess with their emotions.

I can hear Christy and Carri before I see them. That is one of the things I love about the duo. They know how to have fun and are not afraid to let everyone else know they should be the center of the entertainment. Of course, it is natural, which makes it all the more appealing. I don't know what I would do if anything or anyone harmed them.

We immediately go through the requisite I'm-really-okay issue and get down to the real meeting here at The Hole our men. I give them the update on D's fury and we quickly progress to Con. As Christy predicted, Carri is entranced, which surprises me because she is the more cautious of the twins. It seems that Con is a perfect gentleman with an understated sense of humor, good values, wants to be a family man, and has a steady job. Maybe this girl should change jobs from therapy for children to joining me in the P.I. profession. She managed to get all of the information over their first dinner and drinks. Add the fact that Carri thinks Con is handsome with a body to match and the girl thinks she is in love. Wow! It takes just a few more sentences to find out that Con is an officer in the army. Turns out we have a lot in common. He is in the P.I. business too, Army-style. Con is an intelligence officer.

Before I can get more info on this special new guy, some married jerk that thinks he is God's gift to women interrupts us. As I said, it is hard to go anywhere with these two without having some Lothario think they can make some easy time with them. Another lame pick-up line, a hysterical putdown by Christy, seconded by Carri, and a glacial glance from me that would make the icebergs safe, and the louse leaves us alone. Just another girls' lunch out.

Since we have completed the initial evaluation of Carri's love life, I figure it is time to center the conversation on Christy. Why some smart man hasn't locked Christy down yet is unfathomable to me. She has everything a man would want and then some. The problem is that Christy is smart, really smart, and with that comes a wit that can skin a man alive if she is annoyed. I find it the best of qualities, but it has scared off many a man in the past. I've always figured that if that scared them off, then the guy wasn't worth the effort, but the friend in me would love to see Christy in a relationship like the one I have with D. They say misery loves company, but in this case, happiness wants company too. I want Christy to have a guy as great as I do and that means he needs to be just as smart as Christy and just as pretty.

"Christy, I intend to find you the perfect guy. In fact, I intend to make that my next project as soon as I finish this current case."

Christy replies, "Go for it, Rhia! Good luck finding me the perfect man. Do you want me to provide you with a list of all my requirements in a man? Remember, I am not a girl who is easily pleased."

Christy then deflects the conversation right back at me by asking about the case. I told you the girl was smart. Speaking of cases, I tell them that I need to end this delightful liquid lunch while I can still think and drive legally.

I head home to do some more research and have a quiet place to evaluate what little evidence I have. All through lunch, 1.5 million kept going through my brain. It must be the key to the whole case. It can't mean 1.5 million dollars. I could understand that if the case only had Tangy and Todd in it, but I have a third party in play. A million plus dollars would mean everything to a gal like Tangy. She could really outfit herself well with that kind of green. For Todd, it would have meant getting out of debt temporarily as well as providing new gambling funds to bet with for a time. But for Silence Sterling Stockman, that is chump change. Hell, I doubt he would even leave his mansion for that amount. He is so rich, with 75 percent ownership of a pro football franchise, as well as other investments, that one million, five hundred thousand dollars is what he probably spends a week on jewelry for whatever model or young socialite he is currently dating. This has to be the key. I need to find out which lock the key fits. I want to make sure that if I get too close for comfort for the killer, he comes after me. I don't want the killer trying to get to me through my family or friends. I want there to be no doubt that I am the target. The bull's eye is on me!

Chapter 11

Our place makes interior decorators cry. When D and I moved in together, we blended. He brought his favorite things and I brought mine. Together we came up with a style that I call friendly sports chic. We have a couch that has seen many a sports series, the necessary big screen late-model plasma TV, a sound system that screams you are sitting in center court, and two big leather chairs. In fact, the chairs were the only items that we went shopping for as a couple. When we both sat in identical chairs at the store, I knew moving in together was the right decision for both of us. The rest of the decorating can be termed taupe. Taupe is such an ideal color. You don't have to worry about the right accent color or whether it matches the pillows. Plus and probably best when a super-excited sports fan spills beer, nothing shows.

Shortly after we moved in together, someone suggested that we get an interior decorator to spice up the place. The decorator arrived with a car full of binders with color and fabric swatches and I knew things were not going to work out. She took one look around our place and actually got tears in her eyes. Our home was lacking a female counterpoint to the predominant male influence or something like that. Suddenly, she was talking window treatments, hand-painted wall murals, accent chairs, and something call feng shui. I politely showed her to the door and thanked her, but the only time feng shui was going to come into our place was when we brought home Chinese takeout.

I need big-chair time. The purpose of a big chair is to be the one place an adult can go when there are important events taking place. Like when your team is in the playoffs and they are down a great player due to injury or you're sick and don't want to deal with the world. Sunday mornings were made for people who own big chairs. Best of all, the big chair was made for thinking, serious thinking, and that is what I need to do. No phone, no neighbors, no distractions so I can finally get a handle on this case.

Tangy obviously isn't going to give D any more information. The threat of serious jail time for murder doesn't seem to be a concern for her. That has me baffled. D is a great lawyer, brilliant actually, but anyone with any sense of self-preservation would be scared. Every day, ordinary people make up juries. All it would take is some bad juju by one or two jury members and Tangy's apparel will take a decidedly unfashionable turn.

Something big is going on here in our city. Todd Sanchez was a small player. He gambled and lost and I'm thinking that meant he probably owed money to some not-so-nice people. But they are not the types that kill. There is no profit in it for them. The men who lend money to compulsive gamblers do so for the interest they charge. Kill the man who loses and you kill your business. These guys prefer to damage the losers, inflict a little pain to help them gain motivation to find a way to pay their debts. Todd's death just doesn't fit their M.O.

I also can't see Todd's death as one motivated by passion. Todd and Tangy saw each other off and on. It wasn't anything serious. According to what Tangy told D, their relationship seemed more like a friendly hook up rather than an all-consuming love affair. Even if Tangy was dancing with both Todd and Stockman, murder by a jaded and jealous lover doesn't feel right. If Stockman wanted Todd gone from Tangy's life, all he would have to do is open his checkbook and start writing. Todd was a man that could be bought. So why would Stockman bother killing him?

Todd's death was more than a murder. It was a hit. It has every characteristic of a hit. The police haven't found the gun. There is a definite lack of fingerprints, DNA, and any other type of forensic evidence. Todd was killed at close range. One shot to the brain and he was done. Mike said that he had a surprised look on his face. Someone took him by surprise and things happened quickly with no noise to alert or disturb the neighbors. A pro did this, in and out fast, job done. The question is who ordered the hit and why? What was Todd involved in that got him killed? What or whom did Todd know that marked him for death? Was it Tangy, wanting to move up to a mansion? With Todd out of the picture, she would be free to aggressively pursue our rich and newly single football owner? But why would she kill him at the entrance to her own condo? Was Todd even the target? Perhaps, Tangy was the target and Todd got in the way. With the way Stockman's ex-wives hate him, maybe they ordered a hit on Tangy just to get to Sterling. Seems pretty far to go for a little revenge, but that is why domestic issues are the worst. Logic and reason leave the brain when a lover's thoughts of revenge enter.

Tangy is too quiet. I am beginning to think that after Todd's death, she has a reason to clam up. Was Todd's death a warning to keep her mouth shut? One way or another, time is running out for Tangy. I can feel it. The murder occurs. Tangy is arrested. D and I take the case. As soon as I start digging in things that involve the pro football team and Mr. Stockman, my office door gets smashed. The secondary players all seem to revolve around Silence Sterling Stockman. His visit to my office was too quick. He knows something big or is trying to cover up something big.

I said the key to the case was the number 1.5. I need to find the lock that the key fits if I am going to solve this murder puzzle. I am beginning to think that the lock belongs to the flashy womanizer Silence. Now I just have to find out what makes Silence sing.

"Obviously crime pays, or there'd be no crime."

G. Gordon Liddy

Chapter 12

Silence Sterling Stockman needs my undivided attention. I figure he is the type that would like it if I give more effort to watching and talking to him. He is a big player and big players always want to be in the game. No matter how many times or how many different scenarios I come up with, the maze keeps circling back to Silence. I promised D that I would be careful, but a P.I. can only be so careful. There comes a point in every case when you just have to jump into the forefront and make yourself known to all the players. For that reason, I think it is time to reach out and touch good old Silence. I need to find out where he goes, whom he speaks to, which people he avoids, where his favorite hideout is after he leaves the sports complex. Where he is going when he is alone and if he ever is alone. Or does his trusty chauffeur tag along all the time. So game on!

I plan to start the surveillance tonight. I want to follow him after he leaves his office all the way through the night no matter where that leads. This is Tailing and Stakeout 101 and I passed that class with flying colors when I was in school studying criminal justice. I initially took the course just for the fun of it. I figured it might come in handy if I ever had a boyfriend that started acting shady. What I found in the course was a career.

Tonight Mr. Stockman was going to get all my college knowledge coming right at him. I need backup for this. D will insist and so does necessity. Normally, I would contact one of the twins to see if they were available, but not for this night. This would be too complicated for them. I love them and it is great when they go on a stakeout with me, but when I have to do a job that requires tailing someone with multiple cars, I have to retire them.

Never in the history of man have there been two people more inept when it comes to directions. I leave them parked in a certain location. A few minutes later, I call them and tell them to go up three streets, turn right, go two streets, and wait till I reach their location. This should leave them in the perfect location for the person I am tailing to pass their location allowing me to break off. Next, I glance out my window and here come the twins driving right by me from the opposite direction. I spend so much time getting them "unlost" that I usually lose the suspect. No, tonight I need someone a bit more level when it comes to directions and I can't involve D since we might need to bend the law slightly at some time during the night, so I call the very best one after D. I call Ben, D's best friend.

Ben is a rock with character. I met Ben right after I met D and it was easy to see why they were best friends. Ben is loyal, funny, faithful, and always the first one to help D if help is needed. What Ben is not is a boy scout. How could he be when he does the kind of work that he does? Ben loves money, moving it, playing with it, but most of all outwitting anyone who thinks they can get one over on him or outbid him. Ben is a financial genius. D and Ben have an agreement. D's job is to keep Ben's wit, one with a decidedly wicked and uncharacteristically flamboyant tendency, in line and out of lawsuits. In return, Ben takes D's money and makes him extremely rich. I know if I call him and tell him I need him to help in a case for D, he will agree immediately. I just hope his wife, Nikki, says that it is okay for him to join me. I call and leave him a message at his home and, a few minutes later,

Nikki calls back and asks what time and where Ben should meet me. Ben definitely has a cool wife.

First, I head over to my office in steady old Fiona. I have to make a few calls first and check with D to see if there is more information coming our way that might be pertinent for this case. I also need to hit the computer for information for Mike about his daughter's new boyfriend. I sent out messages to a couple of associates of mine who have unique and faster ways to get background information and I am hoping one of them came through with something that will appease Mike. I need to keep him happy if I want to continue having a good shall we say inside working relationship with the police. Finally, I need to make sure my cell is fully charged. It is a minor thing, but the days of walky-talkies are long gone. Today is high tech. If a phone charge goes flat midstream in a car tail, then everyone might as well go home. It's all in the details.

Ben and I agree to meet at nine at The Hole. From there, we will map out the best way to cover our very busy subject. I had hoped to get close enough to his car at some point during the day to place a handy little device on it that would make it easier to tail, but the damn chauffeur never takes a break. The man must be anorexic and have a bladder the size of Montana. Either that or the black sedan that Stockman favors resembles an RV inside. Anyway, Ben and I will have to do it the old-fashioned way, something D would encourage if he were here. He hates it when I invade the privacy of people and trample on their rights. I have to hope that he never realizes exactly what my career entails. If he does, then there is going to be one major fight between us, and I don't want to go there.

Over the past couple of days, off and on, I have kept a close eye from a long distance on Mr. Stockman by sending some business to a part-time associate of mine. I have a casual business agreement with other private investigators in the area. We help each other out from time to time. It is a professional courtesy thing. You never know when you might be working on a case and find out that two of you are on the same case but on opposite sides. Having a good working relationship with the other members of your profession can save time and still allow you to bill your outrageous fees. It is what most people call a win-win situation. From the information we have discovered, I have a general knowledge of our person of interest in addition to his daily schedule. If he is following his usual pattern, then he is at home till ten o'clock. Then it is out to pick up his latest female flavor of the week. Next, they will hit the local hot spots and whatever high society scene is the most important party of the night. I call Ben just to check on his location and progress.

"Ben, I'll head on over to the mansion and I want you to park near the girl's house, but not too close. It shouldn't take me long to reach you once Stockman starts to move. As I told you earlier, the current girl only lives a few blocks away from him."

"Relax. This isn't my first dance with you, Rhia. By the way, I love it when you call and get me involved in shady deals. Lends a quality of excitement to this old settled married man and father of four little kids. Relax, I know the street and I will be there waiting."

"I've been to your house, Ben. With three adorable active boys and one little girl, it is anything but settled."

"Speaking of settled, Nikki wants to know when you and D are going to tie the knot and start having kids so ours have some play buddies."

"Okay, Ben, now you sound like my mother. Your cell phone charged completely? Under no circumstances are you to put yourself into any kind of danger. Just tail when I ask you to, but keep your distance and follow all of my instructions."

"Yes, Rhia and now you sound like Nikki!"

We are traveling in different directions, but are on the same page. I take my spot outside the Stockman mansion and begin the tedious P.I. business of waiting. Right on schedule, at exactly ten o'clock, the gates open and the evening begins. Now we will find out just who has more game Silence or me. You seem to love attention, Mr. Silence Sterling Stockman. Now you've got mine!

"The unforgivable crime is soft hitting. Do not hit at all if it can be avoided; but never hit softly."

Theodore Roosevelt

Chapter 13

Tailing is a dichotomy in the private investigation business. To paraphrase Dickens: it can be the best of times or the worst of times. Tailing is the rush of the hunt versus the loneliness of long hours with only one's own thoughts to keep you sane. In other words, sometimes it's great and sometimes it sucks.

Ben and I have had an uneventful night. I feel badly for Ben. To him, this is a night on the town and a time to let loose from the everyday normality of family life. But Ben's family life is anything but boring or slow. With four kids under the age of seven and three of them boys, Ben and Nikki meet themselves coming and going. I try to remind Ben that P.I. work really isn't all that exciting. Most of the time it is just plain boring. Although this case has had a few surprises along the way, tonight, unfortunately didn't have any.

We've spent the night executing a perfect plan and Mr. Stockman didn't reward us for our effort. He and his latest squeeze spent the evening club hopping. How this can be fun, I can't imagine. I guess it is the duty of the rich and famous to dress up and be seen. Seems like a lot of effort for someone to put out just to get a name mentioned in the next day's paper or some weekly gossip magazine. I guess they do it for the little people like D, Ben, and me. They must think we need the constant news on their lifestyle to keep us amused. I've got news for them. We don't. If all that money just brings them this type of joy, they can keep their money and notoriety.

There is one advantage that I did admire. Not once during the entire evening did Silence and his golden gal have to wait in line. I could get used to having that perk. Pull up to the door of the market, have a cart ready to use, let someone else push it, get your groceries for free, compliments of the establishment, and then exit to the waiting car where your driver greets you and drives you to your next destination. Once there, you again jump the waiting line. That could definitely be easy to take. Still, I don't think I'd give up my ideal life with D in exchange for such a luxury. Maybe yes, maybe no.

I let Ben loose around four in the morning with many thanks and apologies for the boring night. He was a good sport and didn't complain or tell me not to call again. Just a quick "hang in there and be safe" and he took off. Gotta love a guy that flexible. Nikki has a good man, D a great friend, and me, well a great backup for when D and the girls are out of commission. Life is good when you have a crowd like I have. What isn't good is the fact that I am back to square something or other. Hell, I forget what square I am on at this point. All I know is that somehow Stockman has something to hide. I feel it in my gut even if Mother contends that a lady would never have anything as vulgar as a gut. I call it a night and head home or as I think of it tonight: heaven.

D is not waiting up for me tonight. He knows that Ben is my backup, so watching the clock and worrying wasn't part of his nightly routine. Good, I can use another decaf latte and a quick, quiet shower before I call it a day. I'm stressed, frustrated, and briefly consider waking D to see if he is as good at de-stressing as I am, but he looks too comfortable and cute to wake. When he sleeps, I can imagine the little boy in him. Marrying the guy and having a bunch of rug rats that look just like him might not be so bad. D doesn't snore, which is a great plus in a bed partner.

Instead, he makes these crazy noises that remind me of a beached whale. I don't know why I find it soothing. I just do especially after a night like tonight. I watch him for a while longer and slowly my mind eases. The last thought I have before I join D in slumber is that I am sick and tired of dead ends. Tomorrow I come out fighting before I end up with another dead body.

"Perhaps the world's second worst crime is boredom. The first is being a bore."

Jean Bandrillard

Chapter 14

Okay, last night I jumped into the case ready to solve everything and all I got was a sore rump and an empty gas tank. A couple hours of sleep and it is time to get the caffeine flowing in my system again. I'm still frustrated and I hate that feeling. I like order. I like balance. I like when good overcomes evil. I want the world to turn around its axis, Greenpeace to finally stop whale hunts, the earth to cool, and the oceans to stay clear. World peace? Well, let someone else worry about that. Most of all I want a break in this case.

"So how did Ben do as your accomplice in crime last night?"

D's in the kitchen fixing what I hope will be a nutritious, yet fattening, breakfast for me. If I could get by right now with eating a pint of chocolate ice cream for breakfast, I would, but D will have what Mother calls a conniption, which I think means a fit. Then I will get the famous "you need to eat healthier and exercise more." It is not that I need to lose weight or that he finds anything wrong with my body. Just the opposite in fact, D says the first thing he noticed about me were my curves. He just wants me to stay healthy. It is nice to have someone worrying about you, but right now I want instant gratification of some kind. Running two miles and sweating doesn't sound too appealing to me. One of D's great omelets oozing gourmet, deep-yellow Cheddar cheese, crisp, thick-cut peppered bacon, and solid slices of Texas toast slathered with real butter sounds like just the fix I need.

"Ben did a great job, but it was a no-go night. We spent the entire night playing tag and hitting the parking lots of every club downtown. I feel bad for Ben. I'm sure he was hoping for something exciting to happen and nothing did."

D brings a plate that is heaping with an unbelievable assortment of breakfast cuisine to our "formal" dining table. In other words, he put it on the bench in front of our couch that we refer to as our coffee, lunch, and dinner table.

"Thanks babe. This looks and smells delicious and is exactly what I need."

I turn on the TV to catch up on the world news. What did people do before the start of the twenty-four-hour news channel? I wait to start eating until D joins me on the couch because that is what a lady with good manners would do. In spite of myself, Mother's training shines through occasionally.

"D, last night was a bust. I'm sorry that I don't have any more information that could help you with your defense of Tangy."

"It's okay, Rhia. I'd rather you not get information in the middle of the night even with Ben as your backup. Your safety is always my top priority. Besides from what I can get out of the police and the district attorney's office, the case seems to be going nowhere for them as well. The initial arrest was to keep Tangy in town and give the detectives room to maneuver. I think they have had enough time for their fishing expedition. If they still consider her a person of interest, they need to disclose why. Tangy may eventually have a civil case against the police department for arresting her. What is your next step?"

"I'm going to stop by the police station to drop off some information to Mike about another case and see what else I can dig up. Then I think I will go to the office, check my e-mail, and see if I can utilize my computer skills to get additional background on our Mr. Stockman. I especially want to figure out the connection between our three parties beyond the obvious physical one. I just can't get a hold on this case and it is driving me crazy."

"Listen, Rhia, maybe you should just call it a day on this case. If it is a professional hit on Todd, I'm not sure I want you involved anymore. How about you let me handle Tangy's problem and you back off? Can we make this a deal?"

"No way and no deal! My brain wouldn't be able to shut off this case even if I wanted to."

"All right, stay on the case. I have to head to the courthouse now. Promise you will stay in touch and safe."

"I promise."

"By the way, Rhia, I love you and it's your turn to do the dishes. Call me if anything interesting comes up. Deal?"

"Deal and D, I love you back."

D leaves and I finish breakfast and do the appropriate clean up job in the kitchen. Hell I'm so thoroughly housebroken, I even remember to start the dishwasher. That is enough of the Suzy Homemaker routine. It is time for real work. I have to finally earn my outrageous P.I. fees. I can't keep billing D's law firm at my usual rates unless I start producing.

After a quick check of the house to make sure everything is in order, I climb in Bertha and head to the police station. Mike will want to know that his daughter picked a good one this time. Everything that came up on the kid was clean. He comes from a solid family, has above average grades in school, no criminal record not even a driving ticket and even the picture from the yearbook looks good. Mike will have to back off this time and let his daughter have a normal relationship with a guy her own age. It is time for him to cut the strings and let her go. Easy for me to say I'm not the parent. I think I will keep that advice to myself. Mike's temper and his protectiveness of his daughter are legendary. I'll just give him the facts and hope for the best for the poor little girl. The drive to the station gives me just enough time to formulate a few questions for Mike. I just hope this information is enough so that Mike thinks his back has been good and scratched. That way we can keep up the "you-scratch-my-back-I'll-scratch-yours" deal. I could use all the help I can get.

I enter the police squad room and locate Mike easily. He is sitting at his desk with a cup of coffee in one hand and eating something that looks like it was hanging in a vending machine for a year.

"Hey, Mike. How are you doing today? Have you put away enough criminals so I can sleep soundly tonight?"

"Rhia, always a pleasure to serve the public, but since you don't count, do you have my info yet?"

"Yeah, right here. I don't think you are going to like it because the kid is clean. Looks like you are going to have to come up with another reason to keep your daughter locked in her room. Have you thought of sending her to a boarding school or a convent?"

"It has crossed my mind, Rhia, but then I remember that your mother sent you to that expensive, all-girls Catholic school and I figure my daughter would be better off at home."

"Cute, Mike. However, for the record, I only spent one year there and then transferred to public school. Have you got any more on the Todd Sanchez murder?"

"Way to deflect the pass, Rhia. What do you want to know?"

"Everything I can get for free, Mike."

"I know that I don't have to do the never-reveal-who-gave-you-this-information routine with you. The case is at a standstill and the detectives are pissed. We don't get many pro-type hits in our little metropolis and this is starting to make them look bad. The last I heard was that they were interested in 'Moneybags' Stockman and looking into his financials. That's all I've got for you. The rest you will have to earn yourself."

"Thanks, Mike. Say hello to the family for me."

"I will and, Rhia, next time, remember the bagels."

I leave the police station and head toward the office. My cell phone starts ringing and I check the caller ID. I'm not in the mood to talk, so I am letting all calls go to voicemail until I realize it is a call from Mr. Stockman. I hesitate, wondering if we botched the tail and he knew we were there the whole time. Only way to find out is answer.

"O'Neil Private Investigations. How can we be of service?"

"This is Sterling Stockman. I would like to speak with Ms. Rhia O'Neil."

Don't people this rich have other people make the call for them and they answer once the proper party is on the line?

"Good afternoon, Mr. Stockman. This is Rhia. What can I do for you?"

"The last time we met, you said that you would contact the other client to see if they would share information on the Todd Sanchez case and poor Tangy."

Mr. Stockman is being very courteous considering his chauffeur hit the gas pedal hard when he drove off after his visit to my office. I got the distinct impression that he was annoyed with me. It makes me wonder why he is being so polite and nice on the phone.

"Yes, Mr. Stockman. I can remember saying that but with the current situation, I'm afraid there is nothing more to forward to you. Apparently not much has happened since we last met."

"Well, I find it appalling that Tangy has not had her name cleared so she can get back to her usual routine. She does extremely important and sensitive work for me and I need her back at the office. I still want to hire you, Rhia. Perhaps you can find something that will expedite the process. Please consider this offer. I will pay you whatever you want."

"Well, I did complete one of my cases today and I will be able to free up more time to look into Todd Sanchez's murder if you really want me to handle this for you"

"Yes, I do."

"Then I accept, Mr. Stockman. I will e-mail a copy of my

contract, fees, and confidentiality forms to your office for you to sign. I look forward to working with you closely at the sports complex. It is still okay if I stop by there if I have questions?"

"Of course. I will let the security staff as well as everyone else know that they are to give you their full cooperation."

"Thank you, Mr. Stockman, and good-bye."

There is an old saying that goes something like this: keep your friends close, but your enemies closer. I wonder what this new development means. I decided to add him as a client to stay closer to him. The question is whether he is taking the same course meaning he sees me as an enemy now. Maybe I just got the break in this case that I needed. If not, at least it means I will be getting paid double for this investigation. Actually, I'll be getting paid even better than that. I intend to charge Stockman double my usual fees just for wasting my time and Ben's time last night.

Chapter 15

"Good morning, Rhia, my dear!"

Not being a morning person like D, I mumble back something unintelligible, get out of bed, and start groping for the caffeine. D hands me a latte and continues talking.

"Thought you'd like to know that the police officially are cutting Tangy loose today. I just got off the phone with the D.A. and they are no longer calling her a person of interest in Todd's murder."

"Great that means that I have burned two days and accomplished nothing. Actually, D, that change in the situation may help me. So far Stockman hasn't shown his hand. Maybe with Tangy on the loose, one of them will make a mistake."

"You realize that if the police cut Tangy loose, then for all practical purposes, I will be on other cases and you won't have to proceed with the investigation," answers D with what sounds like a satisfyingly smug air to it. However, D is never smug to me because I keep him satisfied and because I know and he knows that I am the best thing that ever happened to him. My reaction to his tone of voice could be because I am not a morning person and frustrated by this case. Whatever the reason, the statement gets my temper fired up.

"Listen if you think I will move on after someone broke my office door, then you are way out in left field and all the hits are going right."

"Relax, Rhia, and drink your latte so you wake up and I get to see the true nature of the love of my life. Don't get mad at me for wanting you to go back to something like tracing overdue books for the library. Remember that I always want you to stay safe and this case had made me nervous from the start."

"Overdue books! Are you asking for a smackdown? Never in my career have I been forced to take such a case. Remember that I am just as successful at my career as you are. I just didn't have the financial advice of someone like Ben until I met you, or I'd be just as rich as you maybe richer."

D starts laughing and I realize again that he is jerking my chain just to get my Irish up. I throw a pillow at him and wish it could be something heavier. I say a few unkind words under my breath.

"Did you say something, Rhia? I couldn't quite catch what you said. Want to repeat that dirty talk sometime more appropriate like the bedroom tonight?"

"If you think that's the way to get lucky, fellow, then you better go back to first base and practice in your mind. In fact, why don't you spend the day thinking about your approach to romance? As soon as I get dressed, I'm heading to the office to solve this case come hell or high water."

"Just wanted to get you fired up for your enemies, love. I knew you'd never walk away from a case until it was over and by that, I mean over to your standards. Just don't do anything too dangerous. Deal?"

"Deal! But dinner better be extremely delicious tonight if you expect to completely get out of trouble."

"I'll have dinner waiting plus I'll add your favorite wine to the menu. Heck, two glasses of wine and I will automatically be out of trouble."

"Smart ass!"

I send D off to work, get dressed, and head to the car. Today is definitely a Black Velvet day. I need to burn off my temper and frustration from the case before I go to the office. With luck, I will be able to take care of both of those with a few turns at ninety miles an hour by avoiding the crowded interstate and taking the country route. I want to talk with the cops, but not until I take my foot off the gas. A speeding ticket now would only give D more fodder to tease me and I really don't want to give him any more ammunition.

After the one-woman race, I definitely have calmed down enough so that I can get to work. I pull up to my office and notice the new door. It is just as ugly as the old one, but I guess I cannot expect curb appeal when my office is a storage center. The more I think about the case, the more I think that the sex between Todd and Tangy had nothing to do with the murder. I figure that it was just a side benefit to the relationship. Just a bit of plain casual sex between two consenting adults. Nothing more. To me, sex is never casual it comes with too many strings no matter what anyone says, but that is just the way I think. I'm not a one-night-stand type of girl. I have way too many nuns in my head for that to happen. Hell, I don't even wear shiny shoes after all those years of Catholic schools. Every time I try on a pair of fancy shiny shoes, I hear some nun telling me a boy can look up my skirt if I buy them. Fortunately, I have gone beyond my saddle shoes days. Although, after the conversation with D this morning and all of his wisecracks, maybe I should get them out just to tease him right back. Then again, maybe I shouldn't. I'm not sure I want to find out if he likes them. Time to clear my head and get back to business. I'll never get anything done if I keep thinking of D and the wine that will be waiting for me tonight.

I call Mike at the police station. I want to know if he has any dirt that he can forward concerning Mr. Stockman's finances. Since Mike is out, I leave him a short, cryptic voicemail and hope that he has entered our generation and knows how to check his messages and return the call. I only say that I want to talk with him. I reveal nothing about the purpose of my call. He will give me the info if he can. Besides, I can't leave a message that implies he is giving me info that the district attorney wants to keep confidential. If I do, I will be out of his favor faster than my favorite basketball player, Manu Ginobili of the San Antonio Spurs, can pump fake to the basket and draw a foul.

As I wait to hear from Mike, I decide to read the local newspaper for any other interesting things on the horizon. I start with the front section and get all the same world news I already learned yesterday from CNN. Then I hit the sports section to see what the local writers have to say about the upcoming football games. I'm about to turn to the comics and horoscopes for a laugh and learn what the rest of the day has to offer me when Mr. Stockman's picture jumps out of the society page.

Someone is proud to announce the engagement of Mr. Silence Sterling Stockman to Evangeline Winston Sullivan of Dallas. Studying the picture, I realize that this is the same young woman that Ben and I watched with Stockman. At least this is good news if Stockman was with her the other night, it means that he hasn't started cheating on her yet. After all, she will be wife number five. With Stockman's record, I hope she has a good attorney and prenup. Maybe I should send her my card and D's card as an engagement present, but I guess that would be in poor taste. I will wait until a few months after the wedding and then drop them in the mail. What this means is that Tangy will not be moving up the social ladder to a higher tax bracket. If she thought she was marking her turf the other night with a late night visit to Stockman's home, then she lost out. That can make a woman mad faster than anything else can.

If Tangy was aware of the impending nuptials, then she was definitely at Stockman's house to discuss business and not the ticket sales type. Either way, this might be the break I have been seeking. Hell has no fury like a woman who thinks she's been had in some way even if she hasn't. The other night may have been a bust, but today is starting to look better and better. I may not get world peace, but maybe I can finally get a piece of evidence to nail someone.

It is time to go visit Mr. Stockman to offer my congratulations to him and his new ladylove. This gives me the perfect reason to drop by his office and, as D would say, snoop around. I will have to remember her name. Don't want to get her name confused with a previous Stockman harem member. Since he was so intent on getting me to represent Tangy, I can let him know that Tangy will be in the clear soon. I'd love to take some of the credit and give him a hefty bill just to see his reaction. Unfortunately, D's "do the right thing" pops into my head. If it doesn't appear that Stockman is going to ante up any new info, I will keep my visit short and sweet. Then I can leave his office and start doing some real investigating. Nothing turns up more information than a few casual conversations with the lower echelon of a business. After all, I have the permission of the boss to hang around and I can fake the smile I need to make people think I am just happy as can be over the news in the paper today. If I'm lucky, I will find someone who is less than happy with Stockman and get some dirt. It is a low thing to do, but I can console myself that I am doing it in the memory of Todd Sanchez. Everyone needs a champion once in a while and I'll be Todd's. I just hope I don't spend the day like Don Quixote, fighting imaginary windmills.

The phone rings just as I am walking out the door. It is Mike and he only has a moment to talk. Seems the financials on Stockman revealed an interesting tidbit. Our rich, newly engaged bachelor isn't as rich as people think. Mr. Stockman made some disastrous investment choices and is strapped for cash. That is all Mike will give me, but it is enough to make me want to get my bill to Stockman as soon as I can. It also means that I may be right about Stockman being less than squeaky-clean. And it certainly explains his latest engagement. If you can't earn it, marry it. When the paper states someone is from the "who's who" of an area, it doesn't mean the place where they live. It implies they have money, old money, money the type of money even the rich wish they possessed. Old money means influence even political influence that can be used to multiply your own wealth just by being associated with them. No wonder it was on the society page instead of the sports page.

This new development gives Stockman a motive to kill Todd if he had something Stockman didn't want revealed. Now I just have to figure out what Todd may have had on Stockman and complete the dots between Stockman, Sanchez, and Tangy. This case might actually be going somewhere. I like traveling and old mystery movies, the classics from the thirties and forties. This case just gave me both. It might lead me to a totally new and unknown destination. To quote Bette Davis, one of my favorite actresses, it was time "to fasten your seatbelts." This ride "might get bumpy."

Chapter 16

I can't help but to get excited driving over to the sports complex. I've been a huge football fan ever since I sat on my father's knee as a little girl and he explained the game to me. There is just something about a bunch of muscular men in tight spandex pants running down the field tackling each other that gets me charged up. D gets a kick out of it when I start describing football in what he calls my "sexy" terms. To me, one of the greatest, purest forms of art is the perfectly executed pass play. To get the opportunity to enter the inner sanctum of the football cathedral well, to me, that is exciting. The fact that I would rather be watching football while drinking a beer on a Sunday afternoon is what D says makes me the woman of his dreams. Personally I think it is my figure, brains, and wit that keep him happy but whatever he wants to call it, I'll take it. It is time to take Silence up on his all-access invitation especially before I hand him my bill and lose this golden opportunity forever.

Never in my imagination would I believe that I could just drive up, park Black Velvet, and enter the complex when a game was not being played. I get excited when we come for a game, but usually our ticket, the ones we buy and not the freebies from Tangy when I'm not around, are so high up that I experience the game through the actions of the other guests rather than the players. Today I will be in the prime seats and watching them up close. It is just a practice, but I don't care. The hell with the case, I just want to spend the next couple of hours being a fan.

If Stockman is involved and wants me to back off, he didn't have to break down my office door to get me off the case. Just the opposite all he had to do was introduce me to a few players and I wouldn't be able to think straight for several days. But Mr. Stockman doesn't want me off the case as far as I know. He has gone to great lengths to hire me.

I wander around the grounds and stadium just to get a feel for it and to maybe have a friendly discussion with one or two of the employees. I luck out and meet one of the scouts for the team. His job is to get information on the other teams they are playing, but today he is observing his own team. I start off the conversation with some general comments about the upcoming games and once he realizes that I'm not a reporter, and that I have Stockman's blessings, he loosens up. We talk about the team, the game, and Tangy. It seems that this guy is single and has a crush on Tangy. This crush must be several months old because he has a wealth of information on our redhead. So much information, in fact, I can almost call him a stalker. If Tangy turns out to be innocent, I might have to give her a call after this case is finished and offer my services to get rid of the guy. For now I just want to pump him for any information that might be new.

Tangy was always pushing everyone in the organization to sell tickets for her. He calls her the queen of ticket sales. She definitely didn't want to stay in the ticket and customer service division much longer. She let on to this guy that she soon would be leaving the organization to go out on her own. She wanted to be the big boss and to work for herself. She never said what the company would be only that she would have plenty of cash to start it. One final thing she said to this guy was that if people thought she could sell tickets now just wait until they found out how good she was at producing tickets for all kind of events all over the world. After that conversation and Todd's subsequent death, Tangy clammed up. Every time this guy started to ask Tangy about her upcoming new business, she turned an angry face to him and told him to butt out of her life and to keep his big mouth shut about her plans.

I change the subject back to what was happening on the practice field. I figure that if I ask too many more questions about Tangy, this guy will get to suspicious and call Tangy to let her know that I am asking about her. I don't want to tip my hand plus I figure that there is plenty more that I can find out through other sources since I intend to spend the whole afternoon here. The way I see it, there is nothing wrong with combining a little pleasure with business. Watching these muscular guys run through their practice is definitely pleasure. I hope that D doesn't mind. Of course, if I come home happy and hungry – and not the kind that wants food he should be pleased with my day's work.

Figuring that his source of information was pretty much now a dry hole, I thank him for the conversation about the team and pretend not to place too much interest on the Tangy story. However, I am intrigued and can't wait to get home to talk with D. I know that Tangy was planning a big score. I need to find out exactly what the score is, who is helping her pull it off, and who is bankrolling it. Could this have been the reason that Todd Sanchez had half of his face blown off? If so, what was the 1.5 million figure and delivery time aspect to the case? Most of all, how were all these things connected?

If what I suspect is true, my D will be back on Tangy's case sooner than he thought but this time it might be for more than murder. This time there will be a litany of charges and someone who cares about Tangy had better start visiting churches and saying a few prayers for her. A Catholic girl like me would leave serious business like this in God's hands.

I'm walking around the complex and so deep in thought that I am not paying attention to where I'm going. I turn the corner and, without thinking, push my way through two metal doors.

Suddenly, I realize that God, or someone, is watching out for me today. I find myself in the center of the locker room and completely surrounded by half-dressed football players. If only the twins could see me now. The wisecracking private investigator is frozen in place and completely tongue-tied.

I need to clarify when I say the football players are half dressed. What I mean is that half the players are somewhat dressed, while the others are naked. I once knew a girl from Great Britain. Her favorite slang word was "gobsmacked." I never knew what that meant until now. Suddenly every eye in the room is on me. I don't know whether to run, stay, or what to do. All I know is that I need to get the dumb smile off my face and remember that I am a pro. D is definitely not going to be happy when he hears this story. Suddenly someone yells that I'm a reporter and men start moving quickly.

"Wait, I'm not a reporter! I'm a private investigator!" I realize that I should not have said that when several players head directly to the door. Others start yelling things such as they didn't do it; they don't know the girl, which guy's wife is on his trail – and while I am still standing amongst a group of half-naked and totally naked guys. Wow. D is really going to be pissed about this! I can't wait to figure out how I am going to gloss this one over because D will know I've done something unusual as soon as I walk in the house. It's the lawyer in him. I can keep things about a case from him, but this is going to be too good a story down the road to keep it quiet for long.

"Guys!" I shout at the top of my lungs. "I'm not here about any of you. I just took a wrong turn."

"Sure as if we haven't heard that one before today," answered a guy behind me.

I turn around and realize that I am standing in front of the star quarterback, who, according to the papers, has an enormously jealous girlfriend. A quick glance down reveals that he is only partially dressed. Okay, I looked. Any girl would and I owe it to the still single women of the world.

"Really. I was deep in thought and took a wrong turn but now that I am here, do any of you know Tangy?"

The quarterback smiles a little too falsely.

"I suggest you leave now before we call security."

I reply with an equally false smile, "I have an all-access pass from the owner so go ahead and call security. I'll leave as soon as my question is answered."

"No problem then, we all know Tangy. She did a good job selling tickets, and we are sorry that someone is trying to hurt her. In fact, if you know anything about it, maybe you would like to share the information now. Seeing that you have an all-access pass from the boss and want to spend more time here with us in the locker room."

Well, it doesn't take a truck to hit me to know that this situation is going bad and fast. I flash a smile, thank the guys without looking back, and leave with as much dignity as I can muster. This isn't how this would play out in most girls' fantasies, but at least I didn't turn bright red and stutter. I have to give myself credit for that bit of dodging and weaving. The excursion is not without some knowledge gained. While I can't say this helped the case in any way, I can confirm to the twins that what all the tabloids say about the naked running back is true. He is all that and much, much more!

"Murder is always a mistake – one should never do anything one cannot talk about after dinner."

Oscar Wilde

Chapter 17

As soon as I enter Black Velvet to head to The Hole and call the twins, the phone rings.

"Hi, Hon! Having an unusual day?"

It's D. Damn news definitely travels fast when you don't want it to fly. I have the feeling that something is about to hit the fan. I hope that D is in a good mood and sees the humor in my latest escapade.

"Hi back, babe! How is your day going?" I reply, hoping to head off what I am sure is going to be a major bit of explaining on my part. Once again, I underestimate D.

"I guess we are going to have to buy a portable GPS device for you to use when you enter large buildings."

I hear the laughter in his voice and take a deep sigh of relief.

"Guess you have already heard about my wrong turn. Who blew me out of the water so fast?"

"Tangy got a phone call from a friendly football player. Said some female walked into the locker room when the guys were changing and demanded to know what they all knew about her. Tangy thought it might be a new detective on her case, but I just had this feeling that you might be involved."

"Am I so predictable that you would just immediately assume it was me?"

"No. Whenever you are involved, I never assume anything. I just know you. By the way, did you enjoy yourself?"

"You will be glad to know that I didn't. First I was gobsmacked, then slightly embarrassed, and then irritated by the attitude of the star quarterback."

"Gobsmacked?"

"Don't ask! In fact, the more I think about it, the madder I get!"

"Okay, now you have lost me, Rhia. You walk into a men's locker room of a professional football team while they are showering after a practice, get up close and personal with some of them, and now you are getting more mad as this conversation is proceeding. Did things get reversed on me again?"

"No, of course not. I appreciate you not blowing this out of proportion."

"Then why are you mad at me?"

"I'm not mad at you, D! I am mad at myself. I left without a single autograph."

"Now I am hanging up. And Rhia?"

"Yes?"

"I doubt if any of them had a pen on them."

Ah, leave it to D to get to the heart of the matter. Now I am sure that I will hear about this for a long time to come.

Before I drive to The Hole, I text the entire crowd for a meet-and-eat. D can wine and dine me at home another night. Thoughts are flying rapidly through my brain, but something the football scout said is sticking. Tangy definitely thought she was onto something big. She bragged too much about being her own boss and worldwide tickets to be small time. Add to that the fact that she shut up too fast after Todd was killed leads me to believe that she is smack in the middle of what is going on in ticket land.

The problem for me is that D is involved. If I tell him this news and he questions Tangy, anything she answers will fall under his stupid attorney-client ethics. If I call Mike and let the police know this information, then I am hurting Tangy's case and my client relationship with D not to mention my newest client, Stockman. I'm between a rock and a hard place. I choose to do what any sensible woman would do in this type of situation. I stop by my favorite shoe store on the way to The Hole. There is nothing like a good shoe-shopping spree to clear the mind.

I buy three hot pairs of shoes that I really didn't need and I have a possible and logical solution to one important question. Stockman wants me to clear Tangy as soon as possible. There has to be a reason that he is so anxious for her to be out of the news. I don't think it is because he doesn't like the effect it will have on the team. Publicity sells tickets and this type of hype doesn't have any hint of negativity such as an injured player or a possible bad trade would have.

Stockman wants Tangy cleared for personal issues and I have a feeling his newest engagement might be the reason for the rush. New fiancées don't want old friends like Tangy hanging around their new boyfriends. If Stockman is short of cash, then a marriage to old money could take care of that in a flash. Doors would open for him so fast that he won't be able to keep up. These doors are the exclusive club type, but not the nightclub type. These have very limited membership and their members have enough money to keep people they don't want out.

I pull into the parking lot of The Hole and kill the engine on Black Velvet. I sit outside for a while and let the cool night air carry the scent of hamburgers and fries to me. I can hear the sounds of the oldies faintly playing through scratchy speakers and smile to myself. I'm glad that tonight is not open mic or karaoke night. Those are the only two nights that I like to hit happy hour, but leave The Hole early. I am always amazed at the way some people think they are talented musically when they should just shut up, but I realize that it is just a matter of taste. Right now, my taste is leaning toward a large burger, smothered fries, and a tasty beer on tap. I know that it will be just a short time before D, the twins, and possibly Ben and family arrive. A few hours with the crowd even though I probably have a full night of locker room jokes coming my way will be a blessing. I can shop for all the shoes I want, but casually bouncing a few thoughts off some of the sharpest minds I know cannot hurt.

After a great burger and many locker room jabs, the crowd calls it a night. The conversation was too light and funny to drop any baggage about the case into it. I can call Christy and Carri tomorrow and D and I always catch up on details at home. Plus, Ben brought Nikki and the kids, so I did not want to start having to talk in low tones or cryptic dialect. The last time we tried to pull that off in front of Ben and Nikki's oldest, he nailed it and we almost blew his birthday gift. So tonight was just for fun.

D and I exchange a quick kiss, say our good-byes, and pull out in our respective cars. I love San Antonio. The city has all the benefits of a large metro area, but you can still find shortcuts to get to open roads. I am anticipating a quick trip home via peaceful country-style roads on a crisp fall night when Black Velvet and I lurch forward and the sound of expensive metals crushing together mars the quiet.

Someone is ramming Black Velvet's back bumper, which means someone is ramming me. I correct the wheel, adjust my body, and prepare to pull over to give this idiot a piece of my mind when I get rammed again. I am in trouble. Deep trouble. Whoever is behind me means to do harm and not just to Velvet. I need to drive, call the police for backup, stay on track, and avoid taking a major hit out here on a totally dark, lonely road. Serious harm to Velvet and I could be stranded with only a sawed-off bat to protect me from whoever is in the other car.

Quickly, I thank the Lord that I am in Black Velvet and not Fiona, but what I could really use right now is Big Bertha. Ram me from behind in Big Bertha and I would just brace myself and slam on the brakes. Bertha is a tank and can take on any car. But I don't have that luxury now. What I do have is speed and maneuverability. I hit the gas and take off glad I'm driving a good old American muscle car loaded with power. Stealing a glance in the rearview mirror, all I see is a dark foreign-made sedan with a crumpled front bumper accelerating. This is going to be a race to see who the best driver is and who has the fastest car. I will have to figure out who is behind me when I have time to concentrate on details. Right now, it is all about the real need for speed and I head directly toward the closest police station.

The friendly lights of our small town are getting closer, but a backward glance shows the car behind me has not given up the chase. I will have to remember for the future not to take back roads when I am on a case. It is a strange thing to think at a time like this, but I guess that is just the way my brain operates. I am not frightened. I cannot afford to be frightened. Instead, I am focused, and I intend to get home safe to D. No loser afraid of showing his face is going to take me out by running me off the road. Strangely, I start singing softly to Black Velvet. I tell her that she can fly and she responds. I knew there was another reason I wanted her other than for her looks. Like every good woman, it is what is under her hood that makes her great and Black Velvet is one great broad right now. I have no doubt that her power is saving my life tonight because I am pulling away from my pursuer. Maybe the car behind is pulling back. Either way, it looks like female power is going to rule the road tonight. I knew earlier that the ride could get bumpy, but I never expected this.

"Murder is terribly exhausting"

Albert Camus

Chapter 18

I hear voices. Lots of voices, all mumbled. Slowly, I open my eyes and glance at the clock. It is only seven thirty in what I assume, based on the sun shining through the curtains, is the morning. My body feels like the time a linebacker playing touch football with me in college got too excited and leveled me with an all-out tackle. It was the last time we let him play and the last time any girls played any kind of football with the first team. It took me weeks to get back to normal. I have a feeling that it may take me just as long this time.

I start counting all the different voices and realize that everyone is here, including my mother and the twins' mother. The twins are here as well and D is trying to keep them all quiet. I am tempted to roll over and to pretend that I am still asleep, but soon I know that I will have to face the music about last night. Some things you cannot put off and your mother's concern is one of those items.

Last night was a long one. After the other car backed off when the driver realized that I was heading very fast toward the police station, I was able to get one last look at the car. The look was unproductive. It was too dark to make out exactly what kind of car it was, let alone get a look at the driver. By the time I realized he was hightailing it back to where he came from, it was too late to turn around and to shine my lights on the car in an attempt at catching a look at the license plate. I was safe and Velvet could be repaired, so I considered myself lucky until I had to spend three hours explaining what had happened to the police. Then again when D arrived. Then again when the twins and Ben and Nikki arrived. Ben insisted that we stop at the emergency room, despite of my refusal, where we spent another three to four hours only to hear that I would be fine, but really sore.

Velvet was in worse shape than I was and that is what hurts the most. My beautiful, sleek Black Velvet's derriere is toast. She is going to need major repair work. It will hurt a whole lot more when I find out that it will come out of my insurance. Finally, just before dawn, I got to take some pills ordered by the doctor and fall into bed. I was too tired to go over the evening's excitement so I promised myself I would deal with it first thing in the morning.

Based on the number of voices and the heated discussion being whispered, I will have to deal with last night, but not the way I want. I want coffee, and then I want to drop off Velvet at the repair shop and go to the office. What are the chances of me being able to accomplish that without a scene? I'd say next to none.

"Good morning, everyone and I do mean everyone, since it seems the entire town is in my kitchen this morning."

"Rhia," Mother screams dramatically as she runs over and grabs me.

"Mom, please not so tight. I have several sore spots from last night, but I am really okay. Why are you here?"

"Someone attempts to kill my little girl, and you expect me and the rest of us to not show up? Really, Rhia, of course we are here. We will stay here until you are all better and promise to drop this case immediately."

I hear groans and realize most of them are mine. Everyone else has gotten super quiet. I don't know what they expect to happen next, but I just grab a cup of coffee and head to the kitchen table. When Mother is like this, it is just best to shut up and listen until she is finished.

After what my head says is several hours, but probably more like a few minutes, she takes a breath, and I get a word into what was a one-person conversation.

"Mother, I am fine. We can't even be sure this had anything to do with the current case. I love you and I am always careful, but I need to head to the office and check all prior cases to make sure everything is as it should be."

"Well, I hope D is going to go with you so there is someone to protect you."

"D doesn't have to go. Actually, my police pal, Mike, is going to stop by several times today. He promised to make his first stop of the day at my office so it will be checked out even before I get there. I gave him a call last night and told him personally all about the adventure."

"Rhia, you call almost getting killed an adventure? Sometimes I really don't understand why you have to do this work. Please think about me. What would I do if I lost my only child, my daughter? Can't you just do divorces or something safer?"

Once again, I take a few minutes to remind her and everyone else in the room waiting to inject their loving two cents into the conversation that domestic disputes can be far more dangerous than any other cases.

"I love you all, but you need to get to your jobs and I need a shower. I will see you all tonight. Dinner here, okay?"

I take off to the showers before anyone can disagree, and I hear them all planning on time and dishes and still talking about my life choices as I start the water in the bathroom. D enters for a quick check to make sure I am okay and heads back to the kitchen to usher everyone out. Then peace, quiet, and hot water! Now I can start to heal and plan my retribution.

Contrary to what I told Mother and everyone else, last night's festivities are definitely about this case. Whoever was driving that car last night knew exactly what they were doing. The police will look for the car, but I'm 100 percent sure that when they find it there will be no prints and it will be stolen. I have obviously hit the ball too close for comfort for someone. My problem is that I don't know how or where I hit the curveball. I am closing in on why Todd was killed and I feel as if I am standing on first base while the third base coach is giving me signals that I shake off because I have no idea whether he wants me to steal or stay on base. My head hurts and it is not from the bumps last night. Before someone attempts to surprise me like they did Todd, I have to figure out what is going on in my world. I sure don't want Mike to have to tell D and Mother that I had a surprised look on my face. I like surprises, but I prefer them to be diamonds not bullets.

I join D in our now-quiet kitchen.

"How did you get my mother to leave?"

"Actually, I did not have to do anything. She made a phone call to someone and then told me she would be back later this evening for dinner and left. I am about to leave too. I want to go to the office. Are you sure you are okay?"

"Yes. I am fine. I am going to my office to think. I promise it will be a quiet day for me." With that final promise, D takes off and I head out the door shortly after him.

Mike is waiting for me when I get to the office. At least I know that he will not hound me to get out of the business. Wrong again. I'm really batting well today.

"Good morning. Pissed off anyone between your house and the office on the drive over here? Have you thought about changing careers, maybe opening a nice coffee, tea, and crumpet shop?"

"Didn't know you even knew what crumpets are, Mike. Thought all cops loved donuts."

"Donuts, crumpets, it's all pastry to me. Want to waste time talking about tarts? I've got some great old time stories about them."

"Funny, Mike. Just what my head needs today, more friends with wit."

"It takes one to know one, kid. Got some information for you. Start the coffee machine and invite me to stay a while and I will fill you in on the latest. Just between friends, remember this is only for your ears, and I will have no idea where you got it. I like your mom and D too much to sit by and watch you mess this up more. I thought I should come by and give you a little instruction on the proper way to investigate."

"Coffee's on and nothing wrong with your ego today, is there?"

"No ego, I just don't want to lose my very own verbal punching bag. Word is that Stockman has an ironclad alibi for last night. He wasn't driving the car, but you have already figured that out. The driver was too good at his job to hang around and see the damage. He knew that it was a miss, which leads me and everyone else, including you, to think it was the same perp who shot Sanchez. Tangy, our favorite redhead, also has an alibi. You've got a third and unknown quantity in the game and suddenly you've become their number one target."

"You're right, Mike. I already figured this out. Got anything else?"

"Yeah, but I'm not sure it has anything to do with your case."

"Okay, I know my head hurts, but you are making it worse. Spit it out, Mike!"

"Suddenly, the detectives are asking about a couple of old complaints about ticket scalping and bogus tickets being bought for games online. Seems like the latest scam is to offer tickets to people online and then when these people show up for the game, the tickets don't work. Tickets are paid for by wire transfers by people who really want to see a big game and are happy to score tickets at any price any way they can. Then surprise! The tickets are bogus and the money is gone. That is the info; I don't know why the detectives are looking at it. Thanks for the coffee. I've got to hit the road. Pun intended. Stay out of trouble and figure it out. I will swing by later to check on you."

"You don't have to do that, Mike. Thanks for the info."

"Actually, I do. Your mother called me before she left your house this morning and made me promise to keep you safe."

"Great!"

"See you later, kid."

"Hopefully not! And Mike, I love you, too."

As my personal policeman pulls out of the parking lot, I close the door to the office, grab my fourth or fifth cup of coffee, and start to do the math. Mike is right. I figured it was a pro, not Tangy or Stockman. Mike knows me and the way I think. Some people call it outside the box, but I prefer to call it my own form of female logic. The answer is right in front of me and I am close, so very close. Otherwise, I would be safe. Remember the basics, Rhia. Two plus two is four. Remember why people do the things they do.

First, Todd gets shot outside Tangy's apartment. They have a "relationship," but I can rule out jealousy as a motive. It wasn't that type of relationship. Second, I tail Tangy to Stockman's house in the middle of the night, but then Stockman gets engaged to a girl with ties to the social register. Both have alibis for last night so they are clear of the hit and run, but not clear for Todd's murder. Third, someone has brought in a third party to eliminate people. Fourth, this third party is new or has been part of whatever is going on here all along yet none of us have cornered the concept yet. Fifth, Stockman wants me to clear Tangy as soon as possible for some reason only he knows. Sixth, my head is starting to hurt again. I am thinking way too hard. Mike implied that I would figure it out and I will. Soon.

Normally I would go for a drive to clear my head, but Velvet is currently indisposed. Plus, if I take off on a drive after last night, all hell will break loose when everyone finds out. I can't go shoe shopping. Been there and done that so I opt for what I really love most. I call D and ask him if he has time for a long lunch.

Normally this would be a long shot, but I think my chances are good today. If I know D, he has already cleared his calendar for the day just in case I need him. I do.

"Truth will come to sight, murder cannot be hid long."

William Shakespeare

Chapter 19

D can cook. I mean really, really cook in and out of the kitchen. Do you get my meaning? My head doesn't hurt anymore and I feel great. Lying prone on the couch, my life is blissful. How one man can take something so basic, so raw, and turn it into a feast that delights all of your senses is beyond me. He calls it light seasoning, but there is more to it than that. It is in the technique. It is indescribable joy. It is reckless abandon. It is totally satisfying. It is the best damn spicy chimichanga in the world. It is exactly what I needed.

I have a full stomach, a clear head, and I feel great. D sits across from me with a self- satisfied smile on his face. Someday I am going to have to use my investigative techniques on him and figure out exactly what he uses and how it is proportioned. A little salt, a touch of pepper, a pinch of top-secret Mexican seasonings, and magic happens. D is a great cook and does wonders with the number of spices he uses. He is the king of balance. D says the art of cooking is all about the number of spices you use times the numbers of pinches, which he describes as a gourmet cook's special type of measure.

"Baby, are you all right?"

Suddenly D's voice has a very concerned tone to it. It could be because I am sitting across from him with the dumbfounded look on my face. Mike was right. I would figure it out and D's chimichanga was just the right solution to all of my questions. Well, not all questions, but the one that has been nagging me for days; numbers times pinches. That is the clue now I need the answer.

"I'm heading to the office, babe!"

"Now, are you sure you are okay, Rhia? Have any headaches? Need to rest? What is going on?"

"I'm fine and you, my dear love, are a genius!"

"That I know but do you have to leave now? What about our long leisurely lunch and you taking it easy for the rest of the day with me? I cleared my entire schedule."

"D, I need to go to the office and go over some numbers and I promise I am fine and will call you every hour. Thanks for the offer of a day off with you, but I need to jump on this thought."

"Rhia, if you are sure you are fine, I'll go back to my office. You will call if you start to get tired or your headache comes back? That is a deal, right, Rhia?"

"Deal!"

I throw D a kiss and take off. I'm on this case like cheese on D's chimichanga. I'm all over it.

I call Mike from the car and tell him to haul his crumpets over to my office. I want to bounce my idea off someone who thinks the same way I do. Mike will keep my idea quiet long enough for me to prove whether I am right. I may not know who tried to run me off the road last night, but I think I know why they tried to. I am close to something big. Now I want to find out who has been hiding in the tall grass watching me while I was hunting in circles. Mike and I arrive at the same time. He takes one look at my face and smiles.

"Guess I am going to take some information back to all those great detectives at that snooty police department today. So have you figured out who killed Todd?"

"No, Mike, but I have an idea as to why."

I spend the next ten minutes relating lunch with D to Mike.

"So D can cook, use a number of great spices, and does something with pinches. What has this to do with the case?"

"Mike, it's the numbers not how or what he used. Numbers!"

"Is this more of your weird female logic? Cooking solves the crime?"

"No. But it might explain the number 1.5 million and why I got run off the road. More importantly it might explain why Todd got shot."

"Okay, Rhia. Explain!"

"Would you kill someone for $1.5 million?"

"We both know that people will kill for a lot less, kid."

"Mike, would you kill for $75 million?"

"If I say yes I would, are you going to call my fellow policemen and end my chance for retirement, Rhia? Where did the number 75 million suddenly come from – outer space or inside your spaced-out head from the bumps you got last night?"

"It came from the clue I gave you, Mike. The one that had Todd's name on it, remember, with Tangy's name as well."

"Yes, I remember. That would be the clue you stole from the crime scene."

"Yes, yes, that one! Mike, the point is the number 1.5 million. Take that number and multiply it, by say, $50. That gives you $75 million."

"Sure, now tell me where you came up with $50?"

"Let's say that is the average cost of a bogus ticket that you purchase online. What would happen if you could find a way to suddenly start offering lots of $50 bogus tickets online? You know, maybe over time, 1.5 million of them. It could add up to a huge amount."

"Rhia, can you stop pacing in front of your desk. I can't follow your story if I am constantly trying to get my legs out of your way. You need a bigger office. Let an old man enjoy his coffee and your story. Sit!"

"Okay, I will sit, but this is really important and could blow the entire case wide open if I am right. Listen, Mike! What if you knew someone who had access to all upcoming events that would likely sell out in the next year? What would happen if you knew someone who might have access to the type of people who like to lend money to people in money trouble? You know the type of people who give short-term loans at high interest? Maybe you come up with an idea to get out of some gambling debts to the people that cover your bets at racetracks. You pitch them the idea that they can make millions by scamming tickets. Then something goes wrong or someone gets greedy and doesn't want to share with others in the scam. It is the numbers. Add it all up and you have a motive for murder. Following me yet?"

"Right I've got your number."

"Hell, Mike, can you ever pass up a pun?"

"Nope! That is why I like you. You even get the bad ones! So you think the detectives are onto a possible motive. That is why they are suddenly taking an interest in Stockman's finances. Take a smalltime scam and enlarge it into millions of dollars. I guess you figure, or should I say, your version of funny math adds up to Stockman as suspect number one. He would have the money to hire a pro and he is not the type to get his hands personally dirty."

"It does always come back to Stockman, but it could be a pro team doing this. We are talking about a lot of money. As I said, it might take someone with connections and I do not mean the social kind. I am not ready to rule anyone out yet."

"Except Todd he is dead, Rhia."

"Well, I do believe in some type of life after death, but I doubt Todd is pulling any strings at this time. Please Mike, no puns here!"

"Well, Rhia, do you want me to convey this back to the detectives?"

"No at least not yet. Give me twenty-four hours, Mike. Let me run with this for a day."

"Okay Rhia, but you have to promise me something."

"What's that?"

"Try to not get your number up for at least a day or two, will ya? I'm tired of talking with your mom every hour."

"It is a deal, Mike. See you soon."

"Sooner than you think. Your mom has invited me to your house for dinner!"

Mike leaves and I pick up the phone for a quick call to Mother to find out whom else she is inviting to the house for dinner. It sounds as if she is inviting everyone I know just because I got a bump on my head. What is she planning, my Irish wake, while I am still alive? I have a case to solve. I don't have time for a party to celebrate the fact that I'm still alive. The question is who is going to win – the case or Mother.

"There's a simple way to solve the crime problem: obey the law; punish those who do not."

Rush Limbaugh

Chapter 20

Mother won. I guess there never was a question after all. I arrived home last night for a full-on dinner and a house packed with everyone I knew. I can't remember everyone I saw, but I now know that if I ever die, lots of people will show up for my funeral. I suppose that is a comfort. Either I was the draw or it was the free beer and great cooking. Now that the people I love are satisfied, I can get back to the case.

D left for the office early today. I decided not to let him know my theory on the motive for the case. Before I tell him that I think Tangy is right in the middle of a big-time scam and murder, I need proof. I may know it in my gut, but the lawyer will want proof. I never let my man down and I'm not starting now. Of course, proving that Tangy is a murderer and swindler probably is not the outcome D will like. That is Tangy's problem, not mine.

I spent time at the football field the other day, but the visit that I intend to make today is only to the paymaster. Stockman needs to explain why he is so hot to have Tangy cleared. This case depends on how I interpret his answer. Piss me off with a runaround and I just may use my baseball bat on his rich society head. I already know that I will not turn my back on him.

Insurance means a quick call to Mike to give him my heading and an "if-I-don't-return" message and I head out the door. Today this ends one way or another.

Today is serious business and that means Big Bertha. No one is going to catch me unaware from behind again. It is offense day. No more dodging and weaving. No more wrong turns into locker rooms even if it would be fun to irritate the quarterback again and scatter the boys. I have fooled around enough and it has not been the fun kind of fooling around. Who is calling the shots on a possible $75 million scam and murder? Stockman? Possibly! Tangy? Well, I doubt that she has the brains to think that far out. Or is it this third unknown player? Time for answers!

Stockman is waiting for me. Never one to leave things to chance when I can turn the odds to my favor, I call ahead and tell the receptionist that Stockman better be in his office or else. He may be rich and one of my clients, but getting run off the road made me mad as hell. My tone conveyed that much information to his receptionist. She obviously passed the message to her boss because he has her quickly usher me into his skybox office.

"Good morning, Ms. O'Neil. I can tell you I am not accustomed to being ordered about by the people I hire."

Stockman is sitting behind his large, expensive desk. He is looking all pompous and irritated. I notice he does not stand when I enter the office or offer me a chair. I guess the niceties are all gone on both sides.

"Mr. Stockman, I told you before my name is Rhia!"

I look directly at him, take a chair, lean back in it, and give him glare for glare before I continue the reason for the visit. I wait until I see him getting ready to speak and then I beat him to it just to irritate him more.

"For the record, I am not accustomed to being run off the road and nearly killed by my clients."

"What are you talking about?"

"Two nights ago, someone tried to use a dark foreign-made

sedan as a weapon. I was the target. Care to tell me what you might know about that before I take a swing at you?"

I watch his reaction to the question. Based on his track record, I doubt if I am the first woman in his life to threaten to plant a fist in his face, but Sterling Stockman is one cool customer, even with the startled and confused look plastered across his mug. At least I got him to drop the irritated look. Fake concern for me has taken over.

"Are you all right? I really don't know what you are talking about today. I can assure you that I know nothing about an attempt on your life. How can you even suspect something like that? I hired you to clear Tangy. Why would I try to kill you? Really, Rhia, how can you even ask me such a question?"

The more he talks, the more his concern for my safety fades. He is getting back to irritated. Well, at least he finally got the name right. I suppose that is a move in a positive direction. Something tells me he is working himself right up into a righteous fit that is going to get me fired. I could not care less about my employment state. I fully intend to bill him heavily no matter the outcome. I want to get all the reaction I can, so I am sure he is not pulling a Shakespeare on me now with the "doth protest too much" routine.

"So, Mr. Stockman, tell me what clearing Tangy has to do with your latest engagement?"

At least that shuts him up for a minute and gives me my second dumbfounded look of the day. It is quickly followed, I might add, by what looks like another righteous indignation storm heading my way. I could say this man is an open book, but I know he could not get to where he is today without negotiating difficult business meetings. I am keeping my offense on the field. I want the ball and he is going to have to hit me hard to take over this game.

"I hired you to clear Tangy because she is a valuable asset to this organization. I did Not, repeat not, hire you to come into my office and question me about my personal life. I suggest you change your tone or you may consider this arrangement terminated immediately, Ms. O'Neil!"

"Back to getting my name wrong again. Sorry to tell you, Mr. Stockman, but once I'm hired, I don't get fired! Especially when someone tries to fire me with a car on a dark, country road. So either you start being straight with me or I will call my police friends and we can do this, not so quietly, at a neutral location. Of course, it won't be so quiet after I call the press and let them know we are meeting there."

"Are you threatening me?"

"Yes, Mr. Stockman, I am!"

"I suppose you think you are the only one with connections at the police station? I can make a call too. You will find that I have plenty of acquaintances that can make your little private investigation business go away. You are out of your league."

I relax further into the plush chair and cross my legs just to show that I am not intimidated. Stockman is out of his chair and is standing stiff with outrage. He is picking up the phone as I answer.

"No, Mr. Stockman, *you* are. I am not like the other women in your life. I do not take orders from you or any other man. To put it in locker room lingo you might understand, I am not here for a pissing contest. I am here for answers and so far you haven't given me any."

He slams the phone down and leans forward on the desk. He definitely wants me to understand what he says next. Emphasizing each word he says, "Don't be vulgar. I have had enough of your disrespect. You are fired. Leave my office or I will call security."

I smile and answer, "Not used to a woman talking back to you? Get over it. I am a private investigator first when I am on a job and a lady second. Fired or not, you are still getting billed and all this means is that you are now suspect number one in my book. That means you will come under my personal scrutiny twenty-four hours a day for as long as it takes for me to get the answers I want. Call your lawyer! Call the police! Get an injunction! Do anything you want! Just know that as soon as I leave here, I am heading to the office of your prospective father-in-law and asking these same questions! Then I will be back to park outside your lot permanently to follow your every move! Remember I am licensed to do this! Have I finally made myself clear?"

I know that I have hit the sweet spot on the bat when Stockman's demeanor changes and he sits back down.

"Perfectly!"

"Great let's begin again. Why are you so anxious to get Tangy cleared? I gather the next daddy dearest hates bad press."

"Your social skills may be lacking, but the answer is yes."

"I assure you that I have all the social skills I need, Mr. Stockman. So how much money do you need to keep yourself as the main owner of this moneymaking machine of a team?"

"If you are implying that I am marrying again for money then you are insultingly wrong. Is it your intention to spend the entire morning insulting me? Is this how you treat all your clients?"

"Mr. Stockman, you are no longer my client. You fired me a few minutes ago. Right now, I consider you what the police call a 'person of interest.' For the record, I couldn't care less why you are marrying. The word is out whether you like it or not that you are short on cash. That gives you a big-time motive for murder and attempted murder."

"I wanted Tangy cleared only for personal reasons. I don't want any scandal to ruin what may be the best chance I have to finally find love. Believe it or not! I do not care. I love my fiancée, Evangeline. I do not want Todd Sanchez's death or the implication that someone in this organization might be associated with his death to ruin what I have with her. Is that clear enough?"

"Clear enough, for now, Mr. Stockman!"

"Then I suggest you leave my office now. Do not call my office and leave an order for me to be here for a meeting. You will not be allowed this access again."

"Expect my bill! I will send a courier with it by the end of the day! Money problems or not pay it quickly Mr. Stockman or I will be back."

"Get out, Ms. O'Neil!"

"The name is Rhia," I answer as I slam the door.

That gets me a smile from the female receptionist. Well, I've learned several things from this encounter. Stockman really wants this wedding to happen. He is no longer my client. Poor D will not be getting any more free tickets to the football games. If I want any additional information about Stockman, I might have to call his receptionist and invite her to lunch. Her smile at me when I slammed the office door spoke volumes. I learned that Mother is right about one aspect of my personality I do like to have the last word. What I failed to learn during this encounter is whether Stockman had Todd killed and whether Tangy is involved? He is still suspect number one in my book. As I said to Mike, it is all about the numbers.

Chapter 21

My drive back to the office started out uneventfully. I checked in with Mike and I told him that I was safe and sound and that he was off the clock. He proceeded to tell me his latest lame joke, and, after I dutifully laughed, we hung up. Why he thinks we both like bad puns is beside me. I would hate to think that in twenty or so years I would be like Mike. Then again, that might not be so bad. He has a great family and a career that has given him satisfaction. Well, until that little shooting problem ended his last stint at the big-time police department. I really don't want to end up with his compulsive pastry eating, which reminds me that it is time to start hitting the salad bar again and stay far away from the beer, burgers, and fries. A girl has to watch her figure whether she likes it or not.

The more I think about my visit with Stockman, the more convinced I get that he has orchestrated this whole mess. Unfortunately, my instinct is still telling me that I am missing something. I would love to have a similar sit down with Tangy but she has lawyered up. Since D is the lawyer and now my only client on the case, that meeting is going to be difficult. I could sit down and irritate Tangy just as I did Stockman. That technique would work with Tangy. I doubt that she has the conversation skills that Stockman has. She is all customer service. Her business instincts are to please, but it could also end up in a catfight if I push to far. I do not want to put D in the middle of something like that. Still, I am contemplating a switch in headings when the phone rings. It is D and, for the first time in our relationship, I actually consider letting it go directly to voicemail. That is not a good sign and one I don't want to start.

"Hi, babe! What can I do for you?" Might as well bite the bullet and hope he doesn't notice the caution in the tone of my voice. No such luck.

"Rhia, baby, what's wrong? I sense a strange tone in that question?"

Blast, what does the man have? Some special lawyer power that can tell when someone is being evasive or does he really know me that well? Does he suspect that I am considering a visit to Tangy's without him?

"Nothing is wrong. Why would you think that? Just having one of my usual P.I. days."

"Now I am starting to worry. Your regular P.I. days recently have ended with you at the E.R."

"No nothing like that. Just got fired by one of my clients. I think you know him, Mr. Stockman. By the way, I think you're going to miss out on future free football tickets."

"That is my girl. I take it you had a meeting and let your Irish temper get out of hand."

"I never let my Irish temper get out of hand. I just let it out to play sometimes. I still intend to bill him. I may even add a bonus in there for me to go shopping on his dime just to make him angrier with me. Care to be my lawyer if we get into litigation or arbitration or whatever you lawyers call it?"

"I am always there for you. No matter what you need! The real reason I am calling is to get a progress report on your investigation about Tangy and my case. I didn't want to mix business with pleasure last night."

"Pleasure! Last night you and my mother threw an Irish wake for me only I was still alive."

"Nonsense. We knew you were still alive although you did look a bit like death warmed over as the night progressed."

"Thanks. Way to score points with your lover!"

"You know what I mean. This sounds like you are trying to, what do you call it, dodge and weave the issue."

"Fine. Do you want a meeting of professionals at my office or yours?"

"Since you are in the car, can you swing by my office?"

"How did you know I was in the car? Maybe I am at the office."

"Sorry, Rhia. You can't pull that one off when you are driving Big Bertha. She makes way too much engine noise to get away with anything."

"I'll have to remember that next time I want to hit the road with a new guy for a weekend and keep you in the dark."

"If I'm in the dark, then you will be right there beside me. Deal?"

"That will *always* be a deal!"

I love that man. Totally! I just don't want to meet with him yet. But when the client calls, even if it is D, I have to act the professional. When working with D in the past, I have always been able to hand him enough information to prove reasonable doubt for his clients. The problem is that I am not reasonable when it comes to Tangy and I definitely still have my doubts about her. It's not a good position to be in when the client is your boyfriend who can read you like a blown play.

As I am driving to my new destination, I give Mike another quick call. I already know how the conversation is going to proceed, but I owe him the courtesy to divulge that I am going to possibly blow him out of the water with the police detectives. Mike will have to know that I intend to explain everything I know about this case to D. Mike will say that he should have known better than to tell a woman something and ask her to keep it to herself. Next, Mike will act as if he is angry with me. I will do the "I am all contrite bit" on the phone. He won't buy it any more than he would buy a bad used car. This is going to cost me a whole lot of bagels in the future. Mike, well, he will do his usual "I'm-just-a-dumb-car-cop-not-a-smart-detective" diatribe if the information gets back to the police station. All will be well at the end of the day. Mike and I will continue our status quo. It is going through the conversation I will not enjoy. I never like to give Mike a reason to be one-up me. He is not the type of man you want to owe. He might decide that payback involves me sitting for hours while he tells me all his bad jokes.

Parking Big Bertha at D's office is like entering a gentle mare in a thoroughbred race. It is definitely out of place. Bertha is kind of like Mother, but I'll never say that out loud. Mother would kill me if she heard that I compared her to a car. Bertha is like Mother in that she is a little worn from age, but still strong and can be counted on when things get tough. Looking around at the other cars, I start to laugh. They are all glossy and new, all status cars, or the latest hybrids. They are going to think that D's girlfriend is down on her luck when they see me exit Bertha. I don't care. Superficial stuff is not my gig. Honesty, sometimes brutal, is what I value. Big Bertha is an honest car and if I need her to be brutal, she can. Now if I could just combine her with Velvet's speed and Fiona's ability to blend into the background, I could invent the perfect P.I. car. This is a great train of thought, but all I am doing is delaying the inevitable. I need to leave my car and face D. As Mother would say, "stop dawdling." Time to get it over. And this day started out so well.

D's office is plush. The walls are covered in a muted gray. The waiting room is filled with overstuffed chairs and soothing music. The art isn't the type you find in hotel, it is real art done by real painters. D is not into superficial stuff any more than I am. I know for a fact that all the art is handpicked by D and is stuff he loves. The man has good taste in his art and his woman. So I ask myself, what is the deal with Tangy?

"Hi. D is expecting me."

Even the receptionist was handpicked by D. While other firms might go for an exceptional beauty at the front of the office, D chose looks and brains. Elizabeth is just as sharp as she is beautiful. I have seen her take a nervous potential client and soothe them until they are as smooth as butter. I have also seen her take an obnoxious attorney from another firm trying to use his best intimidation lines on her. She politely gave him an intellectual putdown that shut him up all while keeping a smile on her face. D pays her well and she is worth every cent. She also knows that I am the only woman in D's life. As I said, D went with looks and intelligence. She motions me to go right back to D's personal domain.

"Your own personal private investigator arriving as requested, sir."

"Such politeness! I know I'm in trouble now."

"Sorry, babe. I wish I could say I am bringing you good news. I hate to disappoint you."

"Rhia, life with you is never a disappointment. I take it you haven't found a good reason for me to talk to the police to get them to announce that Tangy has been cleared of all involvement in Todd's murder and to get them to focus on another suspect."

"Babe, if I could make your life easier, I would. Nothing about this case has been easy or quick. My meeting with Stockman produced some more information and, to be honest, I kind of hope he is guilty if for no other reason than to clear Tangy. I can't say it is definitive yet. Hell, I can't even say it might be possible. I wish you would let me have a few minutes alone with Tangy. Do you think she would agree to a meeting alone with me?"

"Nope sorry! As her attorney, I would insist I sit in on the meeting."

"Blast. It doesn't hurt to ask. Someday I may catch you off guard and get a yes."

"Maybe you will get a yes when you give me a yes to the big question I keep asking you."

"Nice try, Mr. Big Shot Lawyer. I like us just the way we are. If we walk down the aisle, Mother will start asking about grandchildren before the ceremony is over."

"Would that be so bad?"

"No, that would be grand but not in the 'grand' children sense just yet. I will make you a deal. Let's get through this case and then we will revisit the question. Deal?"

"Deal, Rhia. But remember that we will revisit the question especially after your altercation. Now tell me what you can about my client."

D and I spend the next couple of hours going over everything we legally can. Sometimes it feels like a weird dance we are doing, but we both know where our boundaries are. I tell him all that Mike conveyed to me and about my conversation with Stockman. At the end of our conversation, we are back to the beginning. I am still on the case and still need to get more information, but without the opportunity to question Tangy alone. Whatever D might know about his client that could hurt her, he has to keep to himself. D cannot disclose anything that he and Tangy have discussed during their meetings. Those meetings have to be kept secret unless Tangy agrees to disclose those statements to me. It puts me into a precarious position that makes both D and me uncomfortable. Why D is uncomfortable could mean several things. Either I have hit on the fact that he thinks his client could be guilty, but he still has to defend her or he is worried that I could still be physically harmed in some way because of his connection to his client. I don't like either of those scenarios. I leave with a not-so-quick kiss and a promise to be careful and finally head to my office.

Who's on first, What's on second, and Why is rounding third or something like that is an old baseball comedy routine that is a favorite with sport nuts like me. It goes all the way back to before TV, which means it is ancient and completely describes this case. Everything about this case is getting old. All I really have is a possible good explanation for "why," but I definitely do not know who is on first at this point. Earlier today, I firmly promised myself that today this case would be over. I hate breaking promises particularly when they are made to me. The working day is coming to a close for most people, but I have a feeling that this is going to be a long night for me.

"Crime is terribly revealing."

Agatha Christie

Chapter 22

A long night was not in my plan when the day began. Yet, here I am back at my office, twiddling my thumbs and trying to remember that I am an intelligent woman who is great at my job. I can't talk with Tangy and bully her into telling me everything she knows. So far, she has been excellent at keeping her mouth shut. It could be because she is smart or because she is scared and doesn't want to end up like Todd. I can't see her as that smart, so I am going with the scared stupid angle. Also, I am sure that if D thought she was the one responsible for trying to have me killed, he would find a way to let me know. Ethics be damned, he wouldn't sit back and let me get killed. It's not exactly the most romantic way to think about my guy, but it is logical. Stockman didn't exactly open up and help me this morning. A nice confession by him would have been ideal, but ideal things aren't part of the private investigator's life. A private investigator is hired to find out the answers to questions that other people are too afraid to ask or don't want to ask because they do not want to ruin a relationship, job, or something else. I do not have the luxury to be afraid and I am not inclined to act sensitively to others at this time. Besides, sensitivity is not my strong suit.

I spend a little time in self-reflection. I really believe this is all about the money. Most times, when you remove all the peripheral junk, you get right back to the basic--money. It is what makes the world go round not love like the poets and musicians claim. The more I think about it, the more I convince myself that the ticket scam is the motive. That is more than enough money to make anyone's world turn no matter who that person is. Tangy would be the connection because she is already known as the ticket-selling queen. Plus, she has access to all events, not only at the sports complex, but just about everywhere else. It would not take much for her to get all the information one would need to prepare a ticket-selling scam on a large scale. Advance knowledge, good computer skills, and a series of post office boxes is all that is needed. Now that I go over this possible motive more, I realize that you wouldn't even need an organization. Properly planned, a few people might be able to pull this off. Is it really possible that all this is centered on three or four people?

If the ticket scam is the center, then Tangy, Todd, possibly Stockman, and the unknown driver of the sedan are all connected somehow. Tangy and Todd were an item. That much we already know. Todd had a fondness for gambling. Gambling can be fun and innocent, but it also has a hard and not-exactly-legal side to it. Did Todd's gambling addiction lead him to someone who is shady? Did Todd get killed because he introduced someone shady into a ticket scam in order to pay off a debt? That seems logical. Todd had a casual sexual relationship with Tangy whom he met through his connection with our pro football team. Was it just a coincidence that he knew Stockman? Did that relationship include bringing in the main man of the ownership team because he needed some ready cash? Was Todd killed because he was greedy or was he killed because he wasn't needed anymore? Did Tangy shoot Todd to eliminate him so there would be more profit for her and anyone else involved? Tangy bragged about making it big and being her own boss before Todd was murdered. Was Todd killed on Tangy's doorstep to remind her to keep quiet while she still had a job to complete? If so, who was she completing it for –

Stockman or someone else? Finally, what exactly was Tangy doing at Stockman's house the night that Christy and I tailed her? In my line of business, there are always questions and lots of them. What I need now is the single answer that fits all the questions.

Contemplation aside, I need to get to work. I will not get any answers sitting on my backside. Logic says that it is time to tail someone again and see where that might lead me –tonight I decide it is all Tangy's. After my conversation with Stockman this morning, I doubt if he would take the chance on slipping up so soon especially since I told him that he was my number one suspect. The man is too smart for that. Plus, he doesn't want to scare away his latest love or blow his chances at the opportunity his marriage could leave open to him. He did not deny that his prospective father-in-law had the power to sway his daughter away from good old Stockman if he thought it would be bad for his little girl. No, Stockman will play it cool for a bit if he is involved. Since I haven't uncovered the identity of the death driver yet, that leaves me with Tangy. I will have to make a short stop at home to change cars and pick up Fiona. Then I will hit the local gas and food pit stop to get supplies for what will probably be a long night. This is going to be the biggest hurdle I will face. D is going to want to know who I am taking for backup. I am not planning on taking anyone with me. Tonight I fly solo and I can't let D know.

Fortunately for me, D is held up at the office. He left me a voicemail saying that he was working late tonight. I make my stop at home and get set up on my stakeout without having to fudge the story about a backup to D. I hate having to be evasive with him so I just leave a short note telling him what I will be doing tonight. I imply that I will have backup with me. I just leave out who that backup will be. With luck, he will not talk to the twins or Ben tonight. I have not called any of them. If things get dicey tonight, I only want to think about my own safety. After the close call from the other night, I have no intention of involving someone I love in this case. I will not risk their lives. Risking my life, well, that is just part of the profession.

My backup tonight will be Dolly. Dolly is petite, double-barreled, and lethal. She is a Remington derringer. Dolly is also something D and I have agreed not to talk about since we generally end up in a fight about her. I am licensed to carry a concealed weapon as a private investigator. I just prefer my sawed-off baseball bat. Besides I hate guns. If a P.I. ends up in a gunfight, I consider that a failed job. Intelligence and planning are my normal weapons of choice. But then, I usually don't have someone trying to kill me. I may end a case with a lot of people wishing me harm, but generally no one actually tries it. I've got my baseball bat on the side seat and Dolly tucked away near my person just for security reasons. I hope tonight will be quiet, yet fruitful.

Loaded with caffeine, I park Fiona down the street from Tangy's condo. From my vantage point, I can see everyone entering and leaving her front entrance and garage. Slouching down, which is bad for my posture and back, I place a laptop computer between the steering wheel and me, and act as if I am talking on the phone, hoping that will make any nosey neighbor think I am doing some quick work before exiting my car. Thirty minutes from now, it will be dark and I will be able to lose the laptop to get more comfortable. I send a quick e-mail to D to cover all my bases. I let him know that I am settled in for the night and all is well. I hope that he will take me at my word and won't ask for details.

Shortly after dark and just as I am in the middle of an intelligent and interesting conversation with myself about marrying D, Tangy pulls up to her condo. She enters her garage, parks, and then uses the front door to enter the building. I take notice of the fact that Tangy is staying in the areas with the most light. Maybe the girl is smarter than I think. Just as I ponder that thought, a second car that arrives and gets my full attention. I am not the only one interested in Tangy's activities tonight. I may be the first, but whoever is in the second car has taken up a similar spot as me only down the road and on the opposite side of the street. It was the nondescript car slowly arriving and carefully picking a certain type of parking spot that stands out. The driver passed on spots that could be easier to ease into over one that required more effort to park the car. Plus, nobody is exiting the car. Obviously, the driver is so intent on not being noticed by Tangy, he or she is failing to notice that I am watching them. If I had a partner tonight, I would pull out my best Sherlock Holmes accent and tell my Dr. Watson that the "game is afoot." I am in a possible game for my life with the unknown person in the other car and I don't intend to lose.

I watch both the car and Tangy's condo long into the night. Although it is late, I pick up the cell and scroll down to Mike's number.

"Good evening, Rhia. Do you realize how late it is? You caught me right before I hit the sack. Just calling to give me more good news about my professional life. Have you found a way to make things even more complicated for me at my new office?"

"Sorry about the timing of the call. Actually, Mike, I am calling you to give you a bit of information about our favorite redhead. I am staked outside her condo."

"That's the information? I am thrilled. Please tell me that you have your camera and are currently taking interesting shots of Tangy in various states of dress to leave in my car."

"I take it your wife isn't in the room."

"Nope just the opposite. When I told her about our confidential conversation earlier and how you told D everything, she was ready to clobber you. She is counting the days until I retire. If you were taking pictures, I could swing by in my police car and arrest you for being a sick peeping tom."

"Funny, Mike! If you are telling your wife about our confidential conversation, then I do not feel bad about talking with D. I guess I am off the hook with you. Thanks for letting me know. It is such a relief for me. I am calling so late to let you know that I am not the only car staked outside Tangy's condo. Someone else is keeping a close eye on her."

"What?"

"Now that I have your full attention listen. I got here early and carefully picked my spot. Tangy arrived right after dark and entered her condo. Shortly after she arrived, a plain car pulled up and parked on the street. Whoever is in the car is still there and has been for hours."

"You said plain car. Any chance it could be a plain police car?"

"No, Mike. I know the type you mean and this doesn't fit the bill. I took a couple of pictures of the car and I have the license plate number. Can I read it to you?"

"Yeah, read it to me and I will call a pal at the police station and have him run the number. Rhia, who do you have with you tonight as backup?"

"Tonight I am flying solo."

"Good. I don't want any civilians getting hurt if this turns out bad."

"Gee, thanks for the concern for me."

"I know you can take care of yourself. Stay put and I will call you back."

"Oh, Mike, by the way, I have Dolly along for the ride tonight."

"Great. Now I have to be concerned for the civilians again."

"Just call me back with the info on the car, Mike."

I hang up and wait. Thirty minutes later, I am beginning to wonder what happened to Mike when a minivan passes by my car and heads down the road. I love Mike. I wonder which neighbor let him borrow the minivan. The van turns two blocks down and shortly later my cell phone rings.

"Hi, Mike. I love the new family car. Are you and your wife getting ready to have artificial insemination to produce a passel of new rug rats?"

"First, I don't need artificial insemination to produce

anything, kid. Second, I thought I would swing by and get a look at the other car myself. I will give you twenty guesses to figure out what running the plate yielded."

"Well based on past events, let me guess that the car is stolen or the plate doesn't match the car."

"Right on the second part. Those plates belong to a hot sports car. Nobody in his or her right mind would tail or try a stakeout in a sports car and you said it was plain. I decided to do a drive-by."

"Where are you now?"

"I am parked four blocks away. I figured you might need some backup other than Dolly."

"Thanks, Mike. If anything starts to move here, I will call. Are you sure you can stay up late. Don't people at your age usually go to bed by eight o'clock?"

"Keep it up, Rhia, and the next call I make will be to the station to complain about a plain car parked illegally outside my condo and whatever lead you think you might have will be the property of the police."

"Night, Mike."

"Don't forget to call, Rhia!"

"I won't, Mike. Now we wait!"

"Murder will out, this my conclusion."

Geoffrey Chaucer

Chapter 23

After waiting several hours in my car, things finally get interesting. I pick up the cell and call Mike. Just before the call goes to voice mail, he answers.

"Wake up, handsome. I have some news for you!"

"What now! Why are you waking me up? Are you bored again and calling to get some more of my great jokes?"

"Nope, our favorite redhead just entered her garage!"

"Damn, woman! I am comfortable. I guess that means the hunt is on for tonight. Tell me her direction as she leaves the garage and if the other car tails her. It probably will since the creep has been sitting there all night. What time is it anyways?"

"It's just before five in the morning. What is the matter? Are you getting so old that your eyes can't adjust enough to see your watch? Have you thought of trifocals? I hear they can really be a great help to men your age."

"Keep it up, Rhia."

"Hold on, Mike. Here comes Tangy out of the garage. She is in her little red roadster. She is heading your way. And just as we knew it would, here comes the other car right after her."

"Can you get a look at the driver without being noticed?'

"Yeah. Wait, Mike! Guess who is driving the second car?

"Spill it!"

"None other than Mr. Sterling Stockman's chauffeur! Wow. His job really sucks. He drives Stockman all day and then pulls night duty all night. He is keeping a close eye on Tangy's car. I can tell you from personal experience that the girl is obtuse when it comes to people tailing her. Listen, I will give you the descriptions of both cars."

"Hello, has the caffeine gone to your brain? Remember. I drove by earlier and I am a cop. I have a description of Tangy's car already. Maybe I should be the one to tell you to wake up. And speaking of getting your eyes checked, how come you couldn't identify the chauffeur earlier, kid?"

"He had a hat pulled down low over his face. I got the glimpse when he passed under the streetlight."

"Got Tangy. She just drove by and you are right. Stockman's chauffeur is almost right behind her. Going to give him some room and pull out. Are you moving or just sitting on your ass giving directions on how to tail?"

"Are they still going straight, Mike?"

"Yeah."

"Then I am one block away and going parallel to them. Two more blocks and I will turn and take over your position. Tangy may be clueless, but I doubt that the chauffeur is."

"Okay, our pattern is set, Rhia. Keep on the cell and don't blow this. If I even think we are going to lose the second car, I am calling it in. Got that?"

"If I blow this tail, you are free to call in anything you want to your police pals. If I blow this tail, I am heading to another country because I know I'll never hear the end of it from you."

"Just want you to know the boundaries. I may be your backup, but I am still a cop."

"I've got them, Mike. Pull off. I think I know where Tangy is heading."

"Where, Sherlock?"

"She is heading in the general direction of the sports complex.

Want to roll the dice and just head near there and park? I will break off as we get closer and call if they suddenly change directions."

"Your call!"

"Go! Thanks, Mike. I appreciate the help tonight."

"Night's not over yet! Stay sharp and call back."

It is a gamble but one made on an educated guess. With the direction they are heading, there really is not another destination that could fit the bill at this time in the morning. I debate with myself about calling D and letting him know that his client is on another midnight or should I say early-morning drive. Of course, if I tell him that, he will start asking questions and I will have to let him know that Tangy has two tails tonight. Not a good idea. The last thing I need is D rushing in to play the big protector because he thinks I might be in trouble. I do not want him anywhere near this woman. To me, she is too big a risk. D can defend her in court and meet with her in his office, but there is no way that I want D out here in the dark where someone could take a shot at Tangy and hit him instead. I could tell him that Mike is backing me up tonight, but that will set him off even faster. He will automatically assume that it is dangerous if I have a cop as backup. Nope, better not to call D. I can fill him in when everything is over. A few more blocks and I call Mike again.

"Mike, it's me again."

"Were you right?"

"Yes, as always. Tangy is leaving her car and heading into the area where the team offices are located. The woman is so clueless of her surroundings that she even left the entrance gate unlocked behind her. What a dunce!"

"Remember, kid, even a dunce can shoot a gun. Why do you think I was so concerned when you told me that you had Dolly with you tonight?"

"Tell me, Mike. Why do all cops automatically think they are comedians? Hold on here comes our dependable chauffeur. He is hanging back now, but definitely looks like he is going to follow Tangy to her final destination. Blast!"

"Blast what? Rhia? Rhia, answer me!"

"Relax I am still here! Listen, Mike. Exactly where are you parked? Can you see the entrance to the sports complex and offices from your car?"

"Why, kid?"

"Can you, Mike?"

"No, I can't, but I am starting the engine and heading there as we speak."

"Could you do me a small favor, Mike?"

"I don't like the way this conversation is going, Rhia. What don't you want me to see?"

"I am pretty sure that the chauffeur locked the gate after he entered the complex. I really want you to take the long way here. Let's just say that I am closing in on the gate and I may have to hypothetically finesse a lock. You being a cop and all I don't want you around just yet."

"That is it. I am calling it in and getting backup."

"Don't, Mike! All we have the chauffeur on is bad plates. Wait. Let me get closer to see what I can find out. I promise to call if I need back up. Bye."

"I'll be right outside. You have ten minutes. That is all you get. Keep your head down, Rhia. Remember, ten minutes."

Ten minutes may not be enough time to get the answers I want tonight. Mike is going to be really pissed when he tries to call in ten minutes and my cell goes to voice mail. I am turning it off. The last thing I need is for the vibrate noise to echo through the darkness and to give my location away.

I was right. The gate is locked, but for a multimillion-dollar facility, it has a pretty primitive lock. It takes me less than a minute to finesse it. The criminal justice teachers at my college did not teach this to me. This technique is something I have learned over the years. Of course I call it finessing a lock. The police call it B & E--breaking and entering. By my calculations, I have about eight minutes before Mike charges into the fray. Lucky for me, I had that all-access pass for a bit before Stockman fired me. I know my way around even in the dark. People claim the third time is a charm. This is my third trip here. Time to find out just how charmed I am.

"Contemplation often makes life miserable. We should act more, think less, and stop watching ourselves live."

Nicolas de Chamfort

Chapter 24

Usually I like spending time by myself. I have some of my most intelligent conversations when I am by myself. The sports complex just before dawn, I discover, is not that great a place. It is too quiet. Maybe I can use it the next time I am in the mood for a bit of self-contemplation. Until this visit, I never realized just how large this place is. Actually, it is a pretty creepy place even for a professional private investigator. All it has going for it now is lots of long, dark hallways that circle the football field. There are no screaming fans and no vendors hawking their goods. It is like being in a giant mausoleum. Wonderful, now I am having morbid thoughts. I have lost sight of both Tangy and the chauffeur at this point, so I am going to have to take a stab in the dark as to their heading. Mike would have a field day with that thought. The whole P.I. stab in the dark reference could give him a start on at least five bad puns that flash immediately through my brain. What is it about this case that I can't keep my focus? Too bad I cut off my cell phone. I could use a quick annoying call from Mike to keep me on track. An irritating wisecrack about me not being a capable private investigator and I would regain my focus quickly. By my calculations, I still have around six minutes to go until he tries to call me. That should give me about the right amount of time to make my way to my destination even if I am once again in the dark on this case.

Tangy has to be going either to Stockman's office or to her own office. If I had a coin, I could flip it, but I'll just go with my gut feeling now and head to the skybox office. If I am wrong, I will still be relatively close. Tangy's smaller office is just down the hall. I am more concerned with all of us arriving at the destination at the same time. That could be a major disaster. They both could pull out reasonable explanations to explain why they are here. I can't particularly come up with a plausible reason to be here not when I am arriving with a customized baseball bat in my hand. Dolly is back in the car. Hopefully, I made the right choice leaving the little lady behind.

As I approach the area where the offices are located, I can see lights on in Stockman's office. A few seconds later, I have to step quickly and quietly back into a doorway as I finally see the chauffeur coming toward the office from the opposite direction. He is being just as quiet and cagey as I am. Now we have a standoff. He is parking his body down the hall from Stockman's office door and waiting for something or someone. I am closer and can see Stockman sitting at his desk and Tangy is with him. What a surprise! Somehow I need to get a bit closer to the open door to hear their conversation without disclosing my location.

Suddenly, I hear a slight noise coming from a location behind the chauffeur. The noise has also caught the attention of the chauffeur. My guess is that it is Mike and he is making just enough noise to let everyone in the hallway know that there is someone else in the building. I guess my ten minutes are up. I hope his diversion is on purpose. I also hope it is really Mike. Finally, I hope Mike realizes that the chauffeur is now heading his way. If something happens to Mike, I will never forgive myself and neither will Mike's wife. Mike is one tough guy, but his wife is even tougher. She might be the only woman I know that could give Mother a run for her money.

I can slink closer to the office door with the chauffeur gone.

Whatever Tangy and Stockman are discussing is heated. From their body postures, it is easy to tell that the subject of their conversation is making both of them angry. They are seriously intense. I can see that much clearly. A bit closer and I should be able to get a position that will not compromise me and will allow me to overhear what they are saying. If Mike is doing a dance in the dark with the chauffeur, I am going to have to trust him to take care of himself for the next couple of minutes. I am not happy about that, but he is a cop after all. He has more experience than I do. I need to trust his experience. Stockman currently has the floor, so to speak, so I need to just listen to what the man is saying.

"Listen, Tangy, I will not tolerate any more of this. You need to understand exactly who is boss here and who is calling all the shots!"

"After everything I have done for you, I can't believe that you are going to pull out now. I have made you money. It was money that you desperately needed. In fact, you still need money which means you still need me, Silence."

"Don't overstep your position, Tangy. You are not indispensable to me. I can replace you in a second. You do have certain qualities that have made you valuable in the past, but I can find those types of qualities anywhere."

"So you think you can just get rid of me without a fight after all we have accomplished."

"*We* haven't accomplished anything, Tangy. *I* have!"

"Really, you have done all this by yourself. No help from me. Let's not forget all the other benefits I have brought to the table, Silence."

"And just what are those benefits?"

"Our relationship in the office and out of it."

"Hate to tell you again, Tangy, but you are just one in a very large crowd that is getting much smaller now. I think it may be time for you to be terminated."

"What do you think your latest fiancée will say when I tell her all of your activities?"

"Are you threatening me, Tangy? Not a wise move on your part. Whatever happens here tonight will be your word against mine. I figure your word doesn't carry much weight right now. So, if I were you, I would just shut up before I shut you up myself."

"Yes, that is a threat I am making, Silence! I am not about to stand around and let some S.O.B. cut me out of what I was promised! Just try to shut me up!"

Silence starts to stand and I figure this might be a good time to intervene before they start shooting each other like one of them shot Todd. Silence is reaching for something at his side so I charge into the room.

"That is all I am going to take from you, Tangy. You are fired!"

"What did you say?" I yell as I barrel into the room with baseball bat ready. Well, that entrance shut Silence up.

"I said you are fired! What in the hell are you doing in my office, Ms. O'Neil? For that matter, what are you doing at this complex especially with a baseball bat that looks suspiciously like a weapon to me?"

"I'm here because Tangy is here. I followed her along with your chauffeur, I might add."

"My chauffeur? What does he have to do with this?"

"Why don't you tell me? Exactly why are you having your chauffeur follow her? Don't move an inch or I will use this bat on you and I can assure you that I can get to you way before you can get the gun you are reaching for by your side."

"My *gun*? Have you completely lost your blasted mind? I am reaching for my cell phone. I have every intention of calling my attorney to get an injunction against Tangy. I will have you know that, right before you came charging into my office, she was threatening me. In fact, now that I think about it, I fired you, too. I intend to include you in the injunction. I have had my fill of greedy women who think they can drain me of all the money I have."

Damn, I'm back in the dark again and from what I can gather from Stockman, I am about to get sued.

"I just heard you threaten to terminate your lover and moneymaker, Tangy."

"Correction, Ms. O'Neil. I didn't threaten to terminate her. I did terminate her. I fired her. If she expects to get any of the bonus that she was promised from selling so many season passes last year, she can forget it. I also told her to find someone else to cover her bail. I am pulling out. I warned her once before that I didn't want any more bad publicity, but her involvement in a murder case has not ended quickly as she promised."

"Then why was your chauffeur following her tonight?"

"I have no idea what you are talking about right now. I drove myself to the complex early this morning to get work done before I take off for a vacation with Evangeline. Instead of getting my work done, I find myself having an unscheduled and unpleasant conversation with Tangy. Then, you rush in and start asking asinine questions about my hired help."

"If you didn't tell your driver to follow Tangy, then why did he?"

"To put it bluntly since that is the only thing you seem to understand, Ms. O'Neil, how the hell would I know? Now get out of my office. At least Tangy had the sense to leave before I call my attorney. I think I will also make a second call. The second call will be to the police."

I look around and Stockman is right. Tangy has made a quick exit. Suddenly everything is starting to fit, but not in the pattern I was expecting. I wish I could claim that my brilliant mind was able to discern all the evidence and that I came to the right solution to the case after some deep thought, but I did not. It hit me like a shot. Rather, it is the sound of a shot in the distance that brings the clarity. Someone has discharged a gun and I know that it is not Mike. A policeman would not fire first. I take off running in the direction the shot came from, but still manage to get the last word into my conversation with Stockman.

"Call the police, lock your door, and stay away from windows," I yell at Stockman as I start running.

Chapter 25

Mike doesn't have a reason to shoot anyone. He would only discharge his weapon if someone took a shot at him. So the shot I heard from Stockman's office means Mike is in trouble. Based on the conversation I overheard and then stupidly interrupted, I think I will eliminate Stockman from my list of suspects in Todd's murder. If there is a ticket scam going on, Stockman is not in the deal. That man is too concerned about how he looks to his next father-in-law right now. He was definitely shocked when I made my entrance. He became even more confused as I started asking him questions. This case was revolving around his business not the man himself. It is Tangy's fast exit from Stockman's office that causes concern. She booked out so quietly that I did not even notice it. So much for my famous P.I. techniques, when this is all over, I better look into a refresher course. I can take it over the Internet or by correspondence like an amateur. I feel like one right now. Lord knows I can't screw up any worse than I have tonight.

I hope Mike is a man of his word and called his cop buddies before he entered the complex when my ten minutes ran out and he found out that I had turned off my phone. I had two of the players in this game right. Unfortunately, I had the wrong main man. The chauffeur was tailing Tangy to keep an eye on her for himself. Somehow, he is the one who had Todd on the string for betting debts. Todd came up with the idea for a ticket scam and got Tangy involved. The prospect of fast, easy money was too much for her to pass up. He is the one who shot Todd. It was to cut him out of the deal and send a message to Tangy to keep quiet or she would be next. Tangy is nervous now with Stockman pulling his bail money. She has kept her mouth shut, but the prospect of being locked up until this is settled in court and then having a long slammer sentence must have sent her over the edge. She drove here out of desperation. She wanted to be here when Stockman arrived.

She needed to see him before he left on vacation with his new flame. She needs the bonus money that Stockman promised her, so she can get far away. It is the chauffeur. He is the connection I could not figure out even when he was right behind me on the country road. Of course, the chauffeur would know both parties and he knows how to handle a car. This cannot get any more embarrassing for me unless I find out later that the chauffeur also acts as Stockman's butler. All I need to hear for the next twenty years are references to my investigative skills and the murder case I screwed up when it was the butler that did it. Now that I finally have this case figured out, I hope it is not too late.

I'm running toward a gunshot with a baseball bat as a weapon. So much for the theory that if you end up in a gunfight, then you have failed as a P.I. If my stupidity has hurt Mike in any way, then I will quit the business and take up alpaca farming. Mike is out there with someone shooting at him and I am running in to save the day. But I am running blind. I do not know where Tangy is. I do not know where the chauffeur is and, more importantly, I don't know where Mike is. The hell with the noise I make. I am running fast and I want to let everyone out there know that I am coming, including Mike! I just wish I had Dolly with me. I sure as hell hope I hear sirens soon.

Slamming on my brakes, I realize that Mike is okay when I

hear another shot and then a quick third. There is a real gunfight going on now, but at least it tells me that Mike is still alive. The second shot came from a different firearm and direction. Unless Tangy is packing tonight and has turned into Annie Oakley, it means that Mike is shooting back at the chauffeur. I slow down now. Barging into a scene a second time tonight is not going to accomplish anything. Finally, I can hear police sirens in the distance. Either Mike or Stockman has called in the cavalry.

The shots are coming from the football field. Somewhere in the stands down by the field, Mike has taken up a defensive position and drawn the chauffeur down. If I knew that my fellow cops were on the way, I would do the same thing. Mike must have been really pissed when he realized that I turned off my phone. Cops do not follow the same rules that private investigators use. They do not fly solo. They cover their partners and for good reason. Every instinct in Mike told him to enter and cover me and I owe him big time. Now I need to return the favor and cover him. It is back to stealth mode. Without Dolly, I do not have a choice. The last thing Mike needs is for me to mess up his position to the point that he has to uncover himself to shoot and save my butt again.

I quietly move along the wall of one of the entrances to the field and take a quick look. The sun is finally starting to rise. The dawn is helping me locate one person. I cannot see Mike, but I can get a lock on the back of the chauffeur. I guess this is the charm that I am receiving for being here a third time. Mike has to be hunkered down somewhere opposite of my position. Now I have to try to make my way behind the chauffeur before he figures out the perfect shot to take on Mike. I do not have much time. The sirens are getting louder, which means the chauffeur is running out of time to kill Mike and make his exit.

It is hard to crawl between seats in a stadium with a baseball bat. There is no way I am going to try to take out a killer with my bare hands. I will have one crack at him if I jump up behind him with the bat. Without the bat, the law of averages is on his side. I can tackle him, but I don't want to get into a hand-to-hand struggle over his gun. I also don't want to count on getting one clean sucker punch at him before he can get off a shot at me at close range. It is the baseball bat or nothing. He is so intent on watching for Mike that he has not noticed me. I am almost on top of him. Please, Lord, I pray. Just give me a few more seconds.

Whatever I do now has to be fast. I propel my body up. I lunge over the seats in front of me, grabbing the back of the seat to steady my semi-prone body. I swing the hell out of the bat and aim for his knees. Before he can turn, I connect. His cry of pain and a sweet sound that may be a bone breaking are music to my ears. Just for good measure, I stand up completely in the aisle with him and give a second smack down on the arm that has the gun. Fortunately it is enough and he drops it. Not one to leave anything else about this case to chance, I hit him a third time in the stomach just before he crumbles to the seats. I am getting ready for a fourth hit when I hear Mike yell.

"Enough, kid! He is down! Anything more and I may have to take you in for unreasonable use of a weapon and assault and battery."

"Unreasonable? He was shooting at you! He killed Todd! He tried to kill me by ramming Black Velvet twice. I nearly went off the road!"

"A bit pissed off are you, Rhia? I've got my gun on him now and I kicked his gun so hard it is four rows down. Where is the redhead?"

"My guess is halfway across the country by now or at least trying. Are you all right?"

"Yeah, Rhia. I am fine. You?"

"Yeah."

"Good. That means I can ream you good for turning off the phone and not following proper procedures. By the way, if Tangy has taken off, she is not going to get far. Every police car available is looking for her. I called in all the info I had to the station, advised them of what you were up to, and then told them that I was entering to back you up. I left out your lovely breaking and entering bit on the gate. As far as they know, the chauffeur left the gate wide open after he entered.

"The guys at the station ran the info on the chauffeur and he has priors along with a bunch of aliases. He has a nasty past and some equally nasty associates. The detectives found all of my information really interesting. Your theory about the ticket scam and all the movement tonight got their attention. They sent out the forces. I'll have to explain what I was doing helping out a private investigator, but they will get over it once they figure out a way to spin it to the press. They'll probably say that they had it figured out all along hours before you showed up on the scene. By the way, where is Stockman?"

"If he followed my instructions under his desk or in a closet locked in his office."

"Well, at least he owes you. You have cleared him, exposed Tangy, and caught the killer. Maybe D will get free football tickets after all."

"No, I don't think so, Mike. Actually, all D is going to get is to defend me in a lawsuit. I didn't exactly leave Stockman with a favorable last impression."

"Mouth got you in trouble again?"

"Listen, Mike, I almost got you killed tonight. Do you know how bad I feel right now?"

"Not as bad as I would have felt if you hadn't downed the creep with the baseball bat. I am not as good as I used to be at crouching down and keeping low. He was slowly moving in on my position and would have had a pretty good shot at taking me out if you hadn't arrived. Don't ever repeat that, kid, because I will deny it and arrest you for something just for good measure. Whatever you do, do not let my wife know anything about tonight. I have been ordered by her to keep a low profile and not get into trouble. She apparently has big plans for my retirement and our golden years."

"Look here come the reinforcements for us, Mike. It looks like the entire police force has arrived to save us. Mike, if I don't get another chance before the night is over, thanks again. I don't know how I will ever repay you."

"Didn't I tell you? When I retire, I am going to go into business with you. I'm thinking we will call the firm Yackvanovic and O'Neil and move the office somewhere plush."

"Really? Can't I just buy you bagels for the rest of your life?"

"That will be part of the partnership agreement, kid. You show up to the office every morning with my breakfast, a large black coffee and a blueberry bagel with cream cheese."

"You've got this all figured out, don't you, Mike?"

"Down to the case commission sixty-forty split! Your mother was the one who suggested it in the first place after you had the run in with this very chauffeur."

"Great! Do I want to know who gets the sixty in the commission split now or later?"

"Later, kid. It is what you get for having so many people that love you."

"Yeah, I love you too, Mike."

With that we end our conversation. Any talking we do from now on will be to the detectives. It is time to turn on my cell phone and give D a call to tell him to meet me at the station. I hope he got plenty of sleep last night. I have a feeling that this day is going to be long and legally challenging for him. All of it compliments of me.

The uniformed cops immediately separate Mike and me. I am advised to keep my mouth shut and contact an attorney. I am not being arrested, but I will get a free ride to the station. I am informed that I should plan on spending quite a long time there for questioning. One policeman confiscates my trusty bat. I tell them that my car is here, but they do not seem to care. No, it is a free ride in the backseat of a police car for me. Mike is also getting a sweet ride back to the station with one of the detectives. At least the detective is giving professional courtesy to Mike; he gets to ride in the front seat. I get to sit where the criminals sit. It smells bad back here and I am not fond of the steel that is dividing the back seat from the front. I know the doors locked automatically and that I can't open the windows. I tell the driver that I am not impressed with the mode of travel they use for their important guests. I tell them that the least they could do to make my first ride in the back of a cop car more memorable is by turning on the siren. Hell, Mike must be the only cop on this force with a sense of humor. The cop glares at me and tells me that I will get used to it.

I wonder how many laws I may have broken tonight. By my count, none, so he better lighten up or I will tell my attorney that this is a case of cop brutality just to get even. That is another of Mother's favorite sayings: "Don't get angry, get even."

"There is nothing better than an exciting end to a game. Especially if you win."

Rhia O'Neil

Chapter 26

This was a classic murder case. Greed, theft, money, criminals with priors, a sexy woman, lovers, plenty of intrigue, car races, several attempted murder tries, one successful murder, the usual gunfight, and an up-close-and-personal fist or should I say bat fight to finish it.

Case closed for me, but definitely not for Tangy or the creep they are calling John Hockman. That is the latest alias for the chauffeur. Hockman's gun matches the type used to kill Todd. The police will have to wait for all the forensics, but that is just a formality. Both suspects are still with the detectives and, from what I gather, Tangy is singing like a bird with D at her side. He is not going to be able to keep her out of prison. She is going to do time. The negotiations between D and the district attorney's office are to determine just how much time Tangy might do. Tangy is telling the detectives everything she knows and D is doing his best to make it look as if Todd initially got her involved by using her for information about how the ticket process worked.

D is defending her by saying she didn't know what Todd and John Hockman had planned. Originally, Tangy thought the others were going to help her find a way to triple her sales. She thought that she would make lots of money with their help, but she never knew that her newfound friends had included her into the plan to pull off the ticket scam. Unfortunately for Tangy, she went around bragging that she was coming into a lot of money and soon would be her own boss. Add in that nice little piece of paper I found in her condo and her case becomes a slam-dunk for the district attorney. That piece of paper makes it look as if she was right in the middle of everything no matter how she tries to explain it. Her defense is that Todd forced her to continue once she found out what the real plan was. Still, with D guiding her, she might have a chance at a better sentence. It will all come down to how much she can help the district attorney clobber Hockman.

I am exhausted. The detectives are finally finished with me. The story I tell them matches the one that Mike told them so we are off the hook. Well, I am off the hook. Mike is actually getting compliments and kudos from the other cops in the office. I am getting different comments about how lucky I was to have a cop figure out that I was in trouble and that he needed to save me. I was told not to leave town because they may have more questions for me later. I can see Mike and it is really hard for him right now. He is waiting for me to lose my Irish temper. I say he is one more comment away from bursting out in loud laughter.

D takes a break from Tangy's problems and tells the cop hanging around to give me a ride home.

"Listen, I have it cleared from the district attorney's office. Ms. O'Neil is free to leave now and since you didn't let her drive her car over to the police station, you owe her a ride home. I heard about the ride over. I do not want her taken home in the backseat of a squad car. After all she has done to help this department solve this murder case, I expect her to be sent home in the front seat of a car. She is not to be treated as a criminal, but as a valuable citizen of this town. Do I make myself clear?"

A young cop I have never met before answers, "Yes, sir. I will pull a suitable sedan out front and drive her home myself."

"Rhia, I want you to go home and get some rest. I am going

to be here for a long time. No phoning the twins to let them know what just happened. There will be plenty of time tomorrow for that. Rest today, Rhia and don't leave the house. I plan to be home to cook you that dinner I owe you. Plus, I will pick up your favorite wine on the way home. Understand? Today, you rest! Tonight, it will be just the two of us in the house."

"D, I can't sit around all day doing nothing and then let you come home to cook for me."

"Rhia, you can and will!"

"No, I don't think that is fair. I will make you a deal."

"What deal?"

"You can make one of your fabulous dinners and I will spend all day coming up with a great dessert. Is it a deal?"

"You are going to spend the entire day coming up with a dessert?"

"Not just any dessert, D, a very, very, special dessert that will drive you wild with its sweetness and spice. Is it a deal, babe?"

With a huge smile on D's face, I get the reply I was waiting for.

"Rhia, my love that is one deal I will accept without exceptions. Deal!"

I leave D with a kiss that promises that this dessert will be the best he has ever had. The young cop is waiting for me outside the station with an unmarked car. I get in and he starts driving.

"Wow, ma'am, I have never seen anyone get so excited about someone baking a dessert before today. You must be one heck of a baker."

Looking at the very young man driving me home, I am amazed at the ignorance of youth. He obviously has never been in a real love affair.

"Nope," I answer, "I have never baked a dessert before in my life."

We pull into the driveway of my house and I get out of the car. I walk around the front of the car and reach the driver's side window. I stand by the open window to see if the young cop has figured out the cryptic dessert. He stares at me for a few seconds and then realizes just what kind of dessert D is going to get right after dinner. I am still smiling as his face turns bright red from embarrassment. I lean into the car, say good-bye, and whisper, "Sometime in the future, you may get lucky, too. If that happens, send your girlfriend over to me and I will give her a few pointers on dessert."

With his face still red, he thanks me, puts the police car in reverse, and practically flies out of the driveway. I guess I gave him a lot to think about for the next couple of hours. In fact, I think he will be wondering what my dessert is all night long. I hope that it is having the same effect on D.

Time to relax---as ordered by D. Now about that dessert---

Epilogue

John Hockman went to jail for life.

Tangy was fired by Stockman and was sentenced to six years for her part in the ticket scam and as an accessory after the fact on Todd Sanchez's murder.

Mr. Stockman didn't sue me and he did pay the bill I sent. D and I did not get an invitation to Silence and Evangeline's wedding. No surprise there.

D and I didn't send a wedding gift.

It took Mother quite a while to get over my involvement with this case. She still calls Mike to have him check up on me.

Mike got a commendation for his work on the Sanchez murder and still talks to me about our upcoming partnership--- Yackvanovic and O'Neil---just to annoy me.

Carri is in a happy and totally committed relationship with Con.

Christy has just started dating a new guy named Dave. He is a former jock, a dentist, and teacher. On first impression, he reminds me a lot of my D. I am currently doing an intensive background check on him. It is what I do when the twins are involved.

Since Christy and Carri are now dating men their mother likes, she now spends even more time with my mother. Together, they are planning a triple wedding for us.

Every so often, I run into the young cop who took me home in the police car as we discussed my ability to whip up special desserts for D. He still turns bright red when he sees me.

D really liked my dessert idea. So much in fact that it was three whole days and nights before we went back to work.

I am now officially engaged to D, and we are planning a possible quiet summer wedding. Don't tell the mothers.

This case is officially closed.